ESPIRITUS SANCTUS

a novel

by

Sophie Adams

Grosvenor House
Publishing Limited

This book is published by
Grosvenor House Publishing Ltd
Link House
140 The Broadway, Tolworth, Surrey, KT6 7HT.
www.grosvenorhousepublishing.co.uk

This book is a work of fiction. Any resemblance to
people or events, past or present, is purely coincidental.

A CIP record for this book
is available from the British Library

ISBN 978-1-83975-084-7

Written and illustrated by Sophie Adams
with a cover painting by the author.

My book Espiritus Sanctus
is dedicated to my father Philip Le Mercier Adams
and to my mother
Judith Adams and to my brother
Matthew Adams.

Acknowledgements

Thanks go to my mother Judith Adams, and my brother Matthew Adams and people and pigeons.

"The Earth is flat my friend."

The Earth is flat my friend, and when you know that you know everything there is to know about the world.

I still yearn for you, Simon. Burst into tears yesterday evening-over and over again. No one listens to me when I cry! Get your *Despards* on, Ell's; then maybe we'll understand. Life's not that complicated Leon. I'm blaming you Leon, bald head and all for my desperation. Why feel these quadrangles of depth, of torpor, of inertia. Because I'm not being stimulated by anything and at that point I wanted to pick up a brush and paint my way out of this...

God, I'm so desperate to go.

Please make it, So.. I won't know until mid *"Avril"*. I'm listening to Frank Scally on the decks, oh yeah! 'Levoye Brown': bad man, and Tyronne's coming round at 3 o'clock post meridian on the dot with a bottle of red wine. Red preferably, I asked for, all I have is eggs, an omelette and some "Red Velvet" gateau to offer him. Got to pop out for 75 pence tea bags, don't know if I'll make it through the next two hours without goin' to get it. Such are the doldrums...waiting about. Nay! Loitering. Today was physical. The snow's clearing off a mixed bag of straggly rubbish it left behind in its drift. Out here it's mush, all brown. I noticed on my travails from one place to another that the snow was crisper and firmer in some areas than others, particularly in the Richer district; they have clean snow. Like we're flaking off pieces of shit as we go out; the poor, that is. And so I made a coupl'a paintings you know how it is. Ready for an Ambrose Duke to stare at aghast. Perplexed in shock, open-mouthed.. I'm wearing an itchy nylon dress mixed with acrylic it tumbles down round my hips rather ungainfully. It has a leopard print and pearl-drops designed on it.

The trees barked the colours of Christmas. And down Strong street there's a gal. They've turned an angel into a leopard's lair! Geez you alcoholics/bloody men. Well, I awoke in me yolk. You know you can't have a little '*Piece of my heart*' til you blend it blue. So I sent Simon a red letter. Yeowl. Yeowl go away now, won't you- you stupid ginger bitch, what's a man when it's at home? So that was Leon on the ones and two's speed dial as *fuck*. He's got a boat in Tyronne's Yard. Gus and Thali want me perpendicularly exposed as some sort of social sanity unit for the mentally afflicted. Jesus H Christ what's a city if you don't have one? So 'Eye~Sore my eyes reflected in the quadrangle; I am an angel, an eighth grader, two and half I spoke my first word of Erte in a car with my brother looking at shop windows and placards. What's a language if you don't speak Karnak? WTF guys I'm off my Injection! Shurely(!) a cause for celebration? But instead libation after libation was procured because Thali went to "Anglo-sphere" and I didn't and I sat in my D-squared *Despard*-less. And then I met a man. A very kind-of-crippled man whose door I left open and that was yesterday.

And that was in reference to a Job- a means to get money beyond the social parochial control of my mother. I blew it up though, in more ways than one. Preparing food in a caf' isn't my strong-point, to a deadline, no. The man who was going to employ me had the bluest eyes though, sort of secret, unyielding but warm.

6th January 4018: On Permanent

Beyond the dribbles of less than a tenner here and there. I walk a blindline for them and that's at the traffic lights in yellow tinted spectacles; then again I'm wearing them now!

Yonstadt is a shit hole! Full of the specials; its exterior is made of marble, sand and it's terracotta-coloured. It snowed today as it did yesterday and I'm skint. Why apply to anything, what is life but a choice. Affirm I am happy, blissful if not then content.

So I went out: Jesus Christ you ruddy petards get on the computer immediately. When I walk .. I see and understand people and I love them. But then again, there were quite a few men in homeless coats that seemed to say 'Rosie and Sno' to me as I walked past the Cinema. I heard –' *You are the most beautiful woman in the world,*' And actually, what I really want to write down is that a man and his family walked near me, in close proximity to me and seemed to intone.. And actually they were saying something completely different. I walked down the street, in my neighbourhood and I fisted the air. Woo. I think I'm a lesbian on account of the fact that men disparage me so much. And quite frankly, he that talks about suicide to me is covered in the lacquer of low self esteem. Right, the cover may be the revue word that I saw writ' near the Telephone Exchange. Who am I? Am I but a *buttie* wearer who had a 'Dream Before' that I must not laugh my head off at the primates too much, especially as she deviates to buy fishcakes or *shumthing*.. There was a man who I was somewhat forced to 'intentionally' laugh at even though he was miles away. Do people walk around in their houses? I'll eat my shoe.

I'm gonna buy a clown shoe. Just the one, *'Mind'*. There are women that hate, loathe being an understatement. Am I Ruth in the alien corn? Some people look that we "look like a Massifburger". An actual meal. When I went to Arnold's Dispensary, I had to stand in line. But whatever happens at traffic lights in this country dismisses belief! For I am the undercoat and you are the dog- What on earth was Belinda doing in the library? Yes, Colonel-Fry-up, I do declare that if I were to say 'Ella Amnesia' the whole world would open up into some parapraxis of insanity, my whole life would unfold about me. Go and scratch a prison wall with a 50p coin. No thanks, flat, this *isn't* where I feel safe enough to explore everything I ever knew and could know..What is the hairy glove theory.. Well, if I explain that then you'll have me guts for garters, won't you Dr's and Anne. I walk down Lee's Rd, and I walk and think..! In a country under one rule that says I should go to an institution again.

20th or is it indeed nearly the 5th of March.

Why do they –the police- want to section me. Why could they? When I met John, I was unable to sit with him in 'The CAFÉ' because of the way he was dressed, and the fact that he was trying to express that I am mad, insubordinate to him, and uncool. Or was that what his clothes were saying? Or was that the time it took for a relationship to be built? Because, yeah it took a lot for me to go down Habitat Road and walk myself in the same violent place I had howled and screamed and cursed the word that there is a Higher Pow'. I found blessed relief in knowing that God may be female. God resides in all of us. Is my father O being a bad boy in-

Is it a good idea?

Do I have to go suck a stone in the desert again? Do I have to go to the cells again?

Total warrior I am. I love the blood that runs through my veins.Thali rang tonight and at the wrong moment- "Ella was crying when I rang, and I was trying to tell her about money and all the places I'd seen and visited."- Mum, you've got to not know.

God, I love Simon. Certain members of the disclaimer unit don't though. Such as; you covered his eyes. Stop making excuses for that fat and gorgeous bint she isn't your friend, but in the end we love them. I am rigid with fear. Had to hide so much that when I saw the man from the grammar *skool~* I loved him. Blue was the colour of his eyes "Oh~Baudellaire".

When a man comes in to a hospital such as this dressed in some weird outfit and when I say the hospital I mean the world, but I don't really mean the world because I have a feeling my father wanted me to have kids. So I feel guilty about the men I meet.

"They're" turned you into a victim, Ella. For the pain was too much to bear. When I saw her, she carried the Cross. *'Josie'* sucking a clementine, in French. My eyes are for the light but I cannot abide. I cannot stand my feet against this hard wooden floor- and those are jobs they have?! And then I thought of P. Manet's painting, my favourite and the right of a will of a child to have an alarm on their phone as their favourite number.

For tonight I saw two men in black coats stare at a digit. Hadn't it occurred to the famous that we are actually famous, too? There are certain precedents that are required such as?

What are the requirements to be sane, "god" how borin':

1) To feed yourself.
2) To be checked on..
3) To not talk out-loud. To not talk out-loud without being watched by that whore who takes the net curtain down in her back passage alley. Here, I speak of the neighbour diagonally to the left and behind me.

The saddest:

As a man's voice tries to socially interfere with my writing. As I sit in a bed-room and I am watched by a nurse. *I am Ella.* And what I can't talk to my mother? I speak the word that there is a truth and as I listen to this music, I think I am going to a psychiatric ward. You expect me to acknowledge my memories? Hell:- I want to go to U.R or should that be: hell yeah. Or "Fock," yeah. Because the nurse has told Dr P I'm writing a book. Drugs distort what you see:- not smoking cigarettes? Or should that be. *"Let me see what life is like on Neptune and Venus."* A prison song. In psych wards you get given drugs. Or should that be *medication.* Dad, what do I do? You're not there. I am under section..Q) How would you feel? A) It's because I'm not taking the medication that I want to take drugs because I'm not taking the medication. What's abuse, it's psychological. What's psychiatry~ A big P- a way to instigate pain. You can't check up on me all the time- and; also, because my behaviour is so bad. And they had "Loneliness" pamphlets in the Mental-Health shop. And they keep checking on me... And because I'm on a TSO they're going to put me away. Hello Injection GIRL!

2.
In hospital.

"There was a time. When we sat in square cells and waited for time to pass we ate small pots of jam... and chocolate spread and MegaCorps honey and milk that was/ had probably been thru' a homogenization procedure. Something I hated was that there were other people sitting in other cells waiting for time to pass.. until they were somehow cured of their afflictions!?! In another person's eyes I was deemed to be well, but nothing had changed. Perhaps I'd gained weight..? Or the astigmatism had rectified itself but how, in the most non-descript sense; can they tell? When it's not you who knows you inside and out:- It's some gross man who sits in front of you behind a desk or around a table and because of their – *meds*; maybe I talked to them. So high and brittle was my slurred and absconded body..?"

This is a woman obsessed with Conor. And that was writ' on the parochial sub-division in a caf' because he had a penis. And it's a knife edge "Ell's" reality that is? Or is it, and now I'm enclosed in Northster thinking. Anne never said "Nothin" now did she? Silly cow, if only she could stipulate things clearly enough to the doctors she'd be a *Manager*. And for some reason... as I stroked my fair hair I thought write-'amongst many'!! Reasons that is. If I come into the dark of this flat and look through my window at yours across the pedant. I may go into full throttle psychosis. Jesus was a dark man. Wasn't he? Yeah; and I know that to see in the dark first you have to go blind to your own strangeness.

(Delete his name immediately.)

Go into full throttle psychosis if I come into my sensory deprivation unit and not take pine because actually the drugs make me *'try too hard'*; such was the common verbiage in the grocer's shop where I did my shopping to pick up a shit one. I was dressed in a loose baggy coat with not the slightest whisper of a belt. They go in naked.

Q: The most beautiful woman in the world: speech is something we hear but what are words if they're not to be seen. And what are words if you can't listen. And what's hearing a voice?

A: Is that not cantankered down Carson Cross at any point in the specifics of time that yeah, once I was. In Slippage Zoo I ate a chicken and mushroom slice and two boys were sitting at a bench one looked at the other and looked directly at me; because I was swallowing a chicken and mushroom slice, I smacked it right in the gob and looked directly at him.

At the same time: I hear from beyond my window, two blokes – don't get her gender mixed up, will you? A girl and a boy snigger and Hacksaw Bill approves: *Takes a lot to sink a ship,* doesn't it?

Taking drugs that actually constipate you quite virally is ...17:23pm on Saint-Valentine's Day I sat in the Square and did what I loved or should that be the Café and did what I loved but they took the letter E out of the 'Say what You Love' down at the Clifton Ridges or should that be (Country Road) "Pop goes the weasel"(and that's in reference to a lyric etched in stone around a clock tower and weathervane at the top of a fork in the road)- And we all go to work like grafters I fear the Reaper just as anyone does. Stop dissing me... Yesterday I went down. Yesterday I went down the Chowdhury Centre and that Anna didn't take her: 'Coon skin stripe off- might be nice to experience life relatively rather than as a subjective ornament upon the King's dictation that I am: a phallocentric horse whisperer? Man I am in love with a man with mutton chops who wears *Despards*. Take the 'O' out for ovulate-fuck me, no... What's said is real! Everything that happens in mental hospitals is real. Take the keys to see blue skies again and you stop questioning. They must listen, they can't, they shan't. I'm scared Papa. Beauty is not in the eye of the beholder it is in the optimist. Beauty isn't in the Café. It's not in your heart it's in your lungs, it's in the air- written earlier when everything signified psychiatry. A woman hugged me today I burst into tears you give me credit one day.

Here I Am

1) If I were a doctor. I'd link you up to chain you down to set you free.

-They threw a stone outside through the window and now they are making completely shit car exhaust sounds outside that are artificial, mechanic and are designed to scare me and go across my window. You are rude, you have no manners... they are "Barkin' mad" they are egg-hatchers, lice and they are pieces of eight. *Unpleasant people.*

20:47pm

I use my digits. You *stupid* people, I soon realised along with my glass of orange juice that to get over something sad I would have to think about being free and just get on and do things. But who will read it, who cares enough..?For someone, like myself, who believes there is no God, it's a bit hard being stuck with psychiatry. Somewhere on a social contortion Unit called a City. It uncovers dirt from your ears and read you psalms all the way down cocke-addict alley-ways. With no map I found my way and stumble 'til I fall, for there are dark days ahead. Red Russian toad stools, she sits on sometimes I spit the word that there is a God. Curse the day I found her somewhere between the bracken and the rushes-There is a God- Oh yeah? Say that with a mouthful of berries... Your knickers tremble; Diogenes. I am a horse whisperer these days the year is before AnoDomine. The year is someone's. Well, when you're on psychiatric drugs, it's the shit.. It's the *shits* I tell you, Dr. The shits I'm getting- it's very hard to sit still! Sometimes I wish I could have. Smoking helps me to sit, even though it causes cancer. Every time I take one, or swallow one of those many pills, I think "God". And what a great God, he is.

I came off heroin through cigarettes and adrenalin. I am a Cat. Who is G.O.D: I think that he's.. the best taxi-dermist there is? Oh? It's "My life as a cigarette" again, next show on the box, top's this one. "4 leaves left for roll your own's," I sighed. "Right back at y'a." Once there was a raggedy Annie on the lost highway to God's nowhere. And then it struck me down to.-to see you're beauty betrothed..*Like you would do in the Claritin ways*. And so we waited there because Caryatids can't get nowhere, can they and that goes out to the prequel: "When I cross, I go fare thee well" my dear. My chalk eyed;- bitch with black hair scorched-amber eyes, sat there in crimson. Put down your fork and spoon for I am basalt to your shoulder...A white nail actress in this forest of trees! Demonic heiress to a ghost-poet like me. So loose, we dove into lapis pools.

I met Christofur. Those dark days that "Shudder me timbers still".. I dread to think. Sat in Dolphin Square on a black plastic chair beneath a parasol in the drizzle. One hot day in August I'd walked right next to him. He had tattoos of obsolete wars that maybe he'd fought somewhere all 'long his scraggy inked up arms. A face demonically handsome. And he whooped and cursed lurching all the while in Dolphin Sq somewhere between the shadows and the sun that scorched down on our skins... the flavor of raw honey mixed with mango juice. I sat opposite him a good ten meters away and counted days on my fingers for him. Revolted his yearning. Pent up his fury. Scrowled down the battalion lines. And burnt suffocation away. He is a neophyte. Somewhere in a market in Lyndon I carried my burnt and scorched body; cuddled a blanket and braved the street, past the stalls he came to me: fondled my breast; and declared me beautiful. 'Yo' look good.' He said. He kissed me keeping his tongue away..I looked at kiwis, at eggs, at broken cardboard boxes, at hostile glances, at faces swept with hunger and joy. At large women's bottoms all covered in linen, at sari-ed figures, huge men with glinting gold capped teeth, women with ginger hair, women with children; ghostly, pale and straying from their mothers to play with egg shells and feathers. Dust on dirt in that market... Gobbets of blood formed beneath his skin, his cranium; a purgatory! A nether dimension: somewhere webbed and cubic is his brain like little boxes full of sand. Leaking like dreams unrevealed with eyes open, with- the permission of sleep. The grains fall bit by bit- and he plunges deeper past the competition braying-all like mice unleashed. Clad in a black suit and clogs he walks. Then runs, hurtling past the crowds. A Native man selling things watches us,- "*Impermissible*"- he thinks, tall, slender and willowy as he is..We find a place behind a bill-board.. It's raining buckets; I leave him there at the strange furrows, made of cement and brick and plastic. I kissed him. Leaving; velvety tyre-marks on ploughed snow that "*Only poets can reveal.*"

<u>Paranoia:</u>

And you get to save that again by just checking whether it has glass in its ear. Written in Englenike. One lowly Ingle-nook day.

    Rainy-day afternoons jus' ain't mah bag, y'all know? I'm sitting outside and inwards, because a baby is in my body..

Ten to ten, night,~Angelearth.

They hurt me today, in every way, more than once: The bad man in the pharmacy on the Bridge, made me take 'em and he does sew e'ery-day. What is Schizophrenia? But a mustard pot combined in a kitchen called Jasper's and Marie's. They're right behind you on this one, 'coz she is black- what's black but a COLOR I do have pretty *fucking* thickly in this country... The Queen's are pickled in Rohypnol behind a black screen called "Ella"! They drive on different sides of the road... In this Mol-es-ta-ti-on Farm called Indi-GO Bluez. I remember your peacock green eyeshadow..Yeah, and then they moved them plates like the sound they make on the radio sometimes and they rhyme it out " Becca, Sue, and Mary too. God is a black man, for Ella, yes. But we know that Ella is a loud, inconclusive, mess who comes from Go-d-s-v-a-d-i-n-i-a; Goosey Goosey Gander. We have our orders..” said police man 1: what meal- what you like-.. “The perfect nose?”. Roared the Queen’s who allowed people to drive on the left hand side of the road- so they can kill and harass! They’re hurting Cleo tonight by me not being there. Touch… Everyone sit very stiff, with our gas-masks on, Ella’s coming into the room, to be “*Touched*.” Kai RedjamAmys’-son, an authoress: once and once only told me off for not say-ing “Hi” to the guy- Fawkes- from Number 13. Elizabeth spewed her bile by trotting out the Farm today..And the ‘*Woe-be-gone days*’ roared- “We call her Zoe, because she is our Trophy.” And Part the nurse said, in the old days, we used to probe them before we “touched” them “Up.” And up I go and *zo* to bed. What is the point of taking pills to make you normal when no-one else who is normal is taking the drugs. To make the *balance* right? The balance because other people can’t put up with you.

My mum cries herself to sleep every night. Really, why? Because she’s overfed the cat and given it dog’s biscuits instead of cat food. Sometimes, or so it happens I forget that other people can’t do things for me: when it’s only me to answer for, so a man folded my blanket tonight, unbelievable though it may seem, because he was a thrombosis fuck-up called;- Tom…It’s very cold all over the world, for there is no moon tonight. It dangles, sometimes behind a cloud. Why did they send my mum, a text about my glasses? To remind_ME_ to- Standing at the station last night I got asked why & where was “Blanc Lion” Street. I’m leaving the country. You’re going to have to move that old carcass around, m'dear. She, that person that said "El, El, is not coming back." You're trying to assimilate me into your fucking quackery... Pest.. "oleander- fairy...Witch". You should stay it's perfect for your big saucery eyes..The mental hospitals wither and writhe.

Somewhere east of Englenike:

2/11th

Heard my father today, in my prayers. For I am a black one to the river I go. There was a girl called Susannah, on the bus, who was handing out her story. Written in Braille so it seems, as we coyly thumbed the print in woolen gloved hands this being October. The leaves scuttled outside as the little metal ruin made its way. It was pretty non-descript, but she was O.K, and – actually- blind, on the bus.

Sometimes, Freedom tickets & I have one too. Reminds me of Jess Taylor. I'm currently listening to Shaun McStrong singing 'Summer in Jail' he just sang, "The rune is full of rainbows". Sometimes I regret walking down "So_Ho", alone. There are no curtains in Jo's place. Because I hope one day, it will be illegal, to look at people's brains. Especially stranger's.

So, Arkio 'Ateliers'; gave me my phone back- with a broken USB that is sharp and exposes their utter idiocy. I wore a red coat, and there was a man with a port-wine stain on his face. 'A carer brought a so-called: "*beautiful fruit from the strangest tree*" into the Square, a boy with his arms raised above his head, his elbows crossed above his head, and black eyes. Joe was sitting there, the orange man himself; from a Doughty-Place, he saw the child too but he denied it. He's had a stroke, a touch of Cerebral Palsy. So I went to Arkio, today, it was a blazing hot day. And they're going to give me my money; the Government that is. That's what it's like to be poor. And then, later on the same day, I saw a woman riding the back end of a motor bike, clinging onto her partner: a man wearing, like possibly the worst helmet in the history of the world. A white helmet covered in a strawberry design. Which reminded me of a book I wanted to write with the title being "*Le Parfum des fraises.*" About how "Residents of Inglenook" don't understand that fruits smell. Because fruits don't smell until you eat them, do they? Because when you go to the market in Caipur Stream Rd, you understand that, actually-'I stole a strawberry from a market trader's stall.'

I got followed today by an Armenasian. Christ, it was ridiculous, had to pretend I had a knife in the pocket of my red coat. Then outside Copper and Vole, or should that be "Corps and Wall" or should that be "Cooper and World", in Lyndon, two unusual people from a sub-continent were having an animated conversation.

I think to myself, sometimes, I own the birds. Mum, today, said I needed a passport to go to U.R. And what's that if it's not 'Care'. The other day, I mistook a guy standing outside for my father. Because I miss him. My father is dead.

The worst "*woz Northster*" that's where I lost my Square, just get me the Chinchilla fancy pantsy/

31st of October: Tonight I had to pretend my pesto jar was a camera, all night long, because actually the police are watching me? I went to the ''Princes Of Kinnahook'' pub and a dog licked my extremely expensive tights. As I turned around on my way out of the pub, I realised the dog's name was "Ella". The owner looked so disappointed that I hadn't asked the dog's name, as it was the same as mine; but my glasses were broken, and I had mentioned that in my language. I don't have the glasses or the guts for that matter; to put the date on.

$: 4 -Hyroe: They've left all the black and white people I know on my mobile. Since when do I have.. Anne as a friend? I'm locked in *my* Mausoleum of Boredom. Y did I have the Barron Von Munchhausen's.. because that's a housing officer?

People eat glass, they seem to in Lyndon. There are people in fact a group of boys and girls hanging outside my studio, saying "Raise the fire." And that's ridiculous. The IR thinks one man wrote the inter-webs. . What's a Neu-Romancer? Yeah, what is a "Neue-Romance."? Yeah, what is a New Roman Que--- In fact who did this, was it that joonish/omar thing in the phone shop? At school, Miss DeClerc stole my roller skates.

In this country the women are witches and the men are monks. .. "And then I phoned Harry to tell him." They are trying to psycho-pathologise me. The girls outside my studio said to the man with them, something along the lines of, "Plucking a hair from his chin". Except it was said in a vile, twisted, voice, in wack-end.

In hospital under Section 8

Hyper visual contingency plan- I just knocked on a door, they said yeah come in.. And as I opened it, they gasped with horror. And it seemed as though she who was in the tiny room with him … sprayed …they're definitely trying to play it <u>*BACKWARDS*</u>. When I save this document, IT gets measured up..by Soo Heilbright.. they're trying to send me to *"Alonelyisland"*..that's where I draw the line..I got locked in at Arkio for the second time. I call a man's penis.. On Cheynie's *Walk* there's a "Band A-part" happening once a month-it's Really bad P.M.T, Daddy-but what is Pre- Menstrual tension if it's not the fifth dimension..? A memory stick. Robertttt's the tax man. "Are you good at art?" No, I'm shit at art. What's art, it's shit, we play with our shit. What's shit.

Crass.. because people play with eyes? Don't I know, that's how we kill- 'Coz our bodies are full of air.. So we *shit*, coz we get looked at most of the time..which kills! It's soul dispersal..However there is retrieval in the fornication of "One's Own nation"..if you catch my drift. Nah, I'm leaving on a jet plane, and I ain't going nowhere.

In the shower room at the hospital, I cried floods, tears and tears rolled down the very same cheeks that once weren't yours to have. I fed a dying woman the same disgusting tincture that I had been fed by Karen all those years ago.

10/29/13: "<u>No man is an Island</u>", except every man that Ella penetrates with her GOD- like gaze is. They're playing battering rams, next door, the neighbours are except it's one person sitting in a room, on their own.

Eddie and the Moon:

But that Black-hearted-Bitch called Soona, who's married to someone who smokes- And actually that was Antonio's Wine Bar; I went as MolcalmMacLark, and yeah *men* are my "drug of" Choice. "Well, tonight I got molofoyed." And as usual someone knew my name before it was spoken- what's the damned point you excruciatingly talentless pieces of wank from Daddy's wank stain. I'm writing -. "We did our best to make sure she was right handed even though she is in fact a left-hander-wank stain piece of die hard from Daddy's non verbal mattress called the sky. Saw Simon today and he looked like a stiff. Fag butts and 'dat', ''Antonio's the name of a chocolate bar." And Ken-ham-Ian's gone orange. He's in a little corridor called my heart. You're so alive you're skiving the chivey in you, Daddy. In fact, the other night with Nestor was quite interesting, when I called the moon..a ruin. Since when is maize, wheat?? They put that on the Joon-s-Bury-'s plastic bag that I'm eating Tortilla Chips, in fried *Esperanto* called deep Ph-at. Some bloke tried to illicit extreme violence according to my oral expression:-Art.

Actually, inside we are made of solid: air. "Tonight was absolutely hilarious!"Something more significant than that happened tonight. Lyndon respected me for the first time. For revealing its psychosis-Takes some bollocks to spend Halloween anywhere, or should that be in..the Leader's favourite handbag.

There was pomegranate boy, who wore a syringe on his T-shirt at Skimp Fischli's. If there's something women don't like, it's your ability to pacify men? They call her 'Soapi. She swept the floor with the natives in geography. Die.

C'est ce qu'on faits la bas, on appuits sur l'externels.

We live on, in the air that flows around us. I went out that night in my mother's snood and a pair of torn tights on..I was raped externally by 11 ill men and women. Later..Isn't that the whole point of psychiatry to tear a family up, to do everything all for one, one for all. Hooray! And now.

Every day I wake up, I know who I am, then the thought of taking an anti-psychotic every day kind-of-messes things up for me. It's the hardest thing to say, but my mum doesn't want me to take pine. She sticks something in her eye every time I do.

I can't let you know what's going on in my room, she comes out holding a disabled cable, and I hold onto a tissue, really hard and I think, "Shut the hell up, don't go in my room."

A cold wind blows...Coraleyne, my nurse walks in with a face like a wet seal, a sort of underwater pout, a lengthy nose and big wide set lips. She reeks of jobs. She has a gold chain around her neck with the cross on it. I think she will come in to my gas chamber, room number 8, with a wobbly strapped on dildo and try and rape me with it. The dildo would be the same colour as her skin: blue.

I called the one I most love in the world, the one who I love...ugly. Saw her/him standing with their back facing me at a frosty window in the coldest most arid, month.

I have no sympathy for people in Concentration Camps, at least they have work. Or I hasten to add a job. Psychiatry, I invented that word, and now psychiatrists won't stop until I am a psychiatrist.

When I was in psychiatric ward, I listened to the heavily-pronounced illiteracy and fury heavily-sugarcoated in marketed drugs pouring from the music coming out of the television that was covered in a panel of plastic. I. I take pictures of *Doric Columns*. Where are my friends?

What is it that I am catching that I'm not cottoning on to. I sat on some guy's saddle from Dolphin Square who walked me home, strangely enough! I asked him for a cigarette. All men aren't my undercover policemen. Yeah. That's questionable. Because I've had some boy-friends.

Daddy, I loved you.
But not telling me how you got A.I.D.S
Fucked my life up.
Royalty.
<u>Once there was:</u>
A woman who liked the tambourine
The strained sounds of fireworks
Running through her fingers, and her hair too.

We are what we look like, except when we read. Who's parsley, a huge, giant herb growing in your garden. Is that a number 75 bus? No, it's not, I and you will know, when you decide to die, that's why we keep you on pine. No, the answer to that seems to be I am permanently *injustice*. I can do everything better than you can. "Well, in fact if the internet's up and running-it's a good thing." Dream On. There's someone in Kan who's in the hell-hole everyday for not giving daddy blowjobs backwards. Because I didn't watch, *Dorothy*. I'm doing this for every black man that's in a white skin, doing <u>the</u> dance in tassels. I am the effects of the side. Who do you vote for? 'X'? No,*a guv'nor versus a teacher,* in a way, "**Abe Lincoln**" in the end. I threw pine-meds in the pond. "Posted prostitute cards" through the neighbour's post box.

1) Yeah, Mum. Let's go see the "InSane" Exhibition.

Ella is a bit abusive. Mi-ra-Do. Pipi-caca-soso. In a way, it's "inspirotime", I'm waiting for to meet Indigo Cain. Do I have to feel the guilt of other people's tears. Jo's having dinner for supper, except supper's Ella.

Got my tits raped/got my face out, where as it's the other way round for most women. My mum got her button taken away from her, on the rape alarm by the *poleece~*, it's not something she'll confess. She does tend to use words such as <u>committed</u> and <u>convinced</u> around me though...which I find hard to take since I am a convict. I lost my Freedom Ticket, M.C Dawn from the Chowdhury Centre took my right to have one away. This morning I hoped that my mum had taken away the pine from the drawer. Stolen it from her child...This morning, I took it with my tears- this morning at least they were visible. Last night I realised I was some kind of Goddess, cats walk in front of me. I wore a black thing with tassels last night, my "carer" tried it on around her head, she looked like every old-*ish* woman should. I'm sitting in cake heaven, and it's a bit like making biscuits all day…Yeah cookie cutter- Salad bar.F- does she have nightmares in the morning? No, psychiatry didn't like how…we…got dressed in the morning.I love you, because I can't figure you out. What's going on? That I don't know about. . You cannot see the inside from the Outside. I've got Herpes.

What's that layer cake doing here? Your daughter stinks when she comes in our shops. We Geks own Lyndon. We know you stole the wagon wheels. They were a *pound* , sir. Please sir, may I. I had an egg with a honey glaze and didn't brush my teeth, which was gross. After that, Cleo the cat slept in my room. It's Sunday, a definite "Shokran", Fuck You day. R.Legett: said she hoped "Ella, didn't get lost on Green Height, did she?" Green Height is a straight road. Psychiatry is covering up a lie, I created.

The electricity in everybody flows out of Ella. Why? Because she's the darkest thing in the world. I circle… So, life is a semi circle- when you're circling the sick with a man called Simon. Why don't they take photos of models when they're asleep, that would simply be not wrong. Glass broke, splinter in my head- make it bigger in the dump. I wanted kudos, and all I got was coc(k)..cock-ayn.

Downstairs, in the Dark, in Village, they have an office where they keep gerbils in cages for the patient perhaps to occasionally use as therapy. Whilst writing this book I realised that in fact, there are two Darks, or maybe I'm thinking that whilst writing which means I'm editing. I don't like going to the skip, I want to go to the dump, then my mother interjected "You always liked the dump". A book called Ella, well you might as well...Since when? Is **pine** not objectifying, anyway? Wear their skin, see how it feels to bleed from within.

I don't want this leopard print suit:-Sprung Cafe: I sat in, like the worst cafe, but actually I loved the Greezer's. There are kind of hundreds and thousands on your cakes! Yeah, yeah I screamed/rather shouted at my mum..again. Since when do I hang out with quietly unattractive people? And, I decided that actually I would rethink my look. Since I am no longer smoking. I love "Z'EEN" Road. And then I realised I felt better, I had been there before, and as well I didn't *really acknowledge that myself*. A guy at the bus stop, kind of aimed for the glass screen in front of me! I like peop's that don't have to show their religion. It's the same in all cultures. God, I guess I'll miss out on the bluebo' gateau. I'm sitting in cake heaven, and it's a bit like making biscuits all day."Yeah cookie cutter"- salad bar.

"Do you hear voices in water?" and I say "No, I'm more of a cover my ears, girl." And yeah that's what a scientist asked me? It's a stupid theory, but when I hear screaming in the middle of the night, pop a pill, it's over. You re-arrange people's doors in this country. You put Choco-Leibchen, in my studio. You estrange me. You re-arrange. Republic, go back to the lunatic asylum, you don't know what a moon is.

"*Shokran*—Go to Hell/ Go to Hell~*Shokran*"

I'm not a crazy girl, but I don't know anyone that is.... because actually I'm worried about money. When you read things out of context, I'm not anyone's daughter-you took away my right to revile.-Yeah-.So, what's wrong with smoking. So much. The cat doesn't like it. And yeah, I smoked crack too; with some guy. Man, I can't even write his name into my book. He touched me up afterwards, and yeah, there's a silver "foil" sculpture hangin' from the ceilin' in 'Sois Sage', and there's two giants kissing. And, I read into things.

You don't need crack to find love. What's that guy doin' smoking crack? What's that guy doing smoking from a biro? Who cares, but when I smoked it, I thought I could fly. But then, again; when I trod on some glass I flew up the stairs. Today, I thought I was an index? Boy, that's so bad it's good. What's slavery all about? This guy, Jonny, took my hand, made me touch his wife's arm, it was the colour of gold, and...This bitch, Jo, sat and smirked in the background. Man, they had a party, the crack guy walks in through the sliding doors, the wife's in there, their kid walks off with my phone.

Then, their kid's boots are left on the top of the sofa. What's going on that I don't know about? What are objects if they're not words? And that's when I knew that if I couldn't write your real name in my book, I didn't want to know you. And yet, smoke drugs with someone:- get to know 'em. That's so bad, it's not true.

<u>I lose my glasses:</u>

There's a lemon in my room for a reason. Yesterday I was holding my shit little mobile, leaning against some rails, I looked left, a *wooo*-man was walking behind me, and I turned slightly right still holding my mobile pointed my index finger at her and screamed at her "You". I felt like shit after that and walked home, somewhere, up Five Fathoms. This morning, sitting opposite the lemon, I'm listening to a station on the radio, NansieBoi's playing, it's a bad song, I turn the dial, because I'd rather listen to white noise. Smoke crack with a guy..Apparently it's Wednesday- it's "A" day. Yeah right, better wear my pants, as always. Some blonde comes on the radio- man, it's a bad song, but it's soo good!

OK, lose this scenario, better get to Arkio. What does psychiatry mean? "I forget things now." But all I wanted was to remember to forget. My brother's having a baby. His partner's called Sian! Boy, man, give it a joint, it's a "Marley..." Yep, little drugs bunny that it might be. It's all about yellow socks. Yeah right! Bit of a brief one but I'll explain it later. You think that's funny, you astro-nomist gone wrong- sitting in a queue wearing leggings that don't fit you. What's lint. What's a ward-round, it's a straight thing---- who's your dad, we don't know him, yet! Sounds and directions have evaded me all my life.

I'll give them one thing, and one thing (only) they're good at words. They took my explicitness away, what's explicitness, it's sexual. That is the living proof I am not schizophrenic. We're in denial in this **Cunt**-ree- I hear thoughts in the movement of objects.. but certainly not in water. That's nothing. Robertttt. I'm going to where the cigarettes are. If anybody, it was not my *bredrin*, but in a way that's a brother, if you don't have one.

I knew, this day would come, I looked at my computer, knew I was writing a book, and it wasn't in the right

order. Robertttt, look what happened to your sister. Man/
woman, I can't fuck her now. What's hate? Bequeath. We
have no money, because my mum was too generous with
my brother. Your daughter's an actress now, too many
people tried to *bequeath* her- too many people tried to
live in her body. Yeah, my brother- something did happen
to my sense of suspension, I need to move around a lot.
You look weird in photos-by the way. What are saints?
Psychiatrists, what's a scientist? All.

Yeah, I do have a mental health problem, but once I
didn't. I thought that when I sat down, looked up and a
bird flew above my head as I looked up through the
window.

Wisdom means thought. My brother's real name is ''
To me, it does." He lives in Amway.

LOOKING FOR A DEAD MAN.

''My brother liked reading in the tent in the garden,
he always liked tents."

Anne, lick the fungus off my feet-And in a way, when I
read that back to myself, I thought that it read to me like
me trying to fight my way back to freedom. What did my
brother do to that dog at home? Why did that dog look
so ill! Animals are ill, humans get sick. Every time I look
at men, I suppose it's supposed to be an admonishment.

Robertttt, although you are in "another country" I
like stars too. Hey, where in a restaurant, the waitress
comes over, says "Ok, guys, who's paying?" I think to
myself and say; "Well, I pay for the whole family."
Yeah, that old joke, I hit the sofa, I mean who cares!
Me. It's a rock, like stone, you're swallowing stones!

You don't think it affects people, of course- who are the sides...You eat your family? Yeah we're all cannibals, here. But where's here, when a giant muscular woman walks in takes your memories out- gives you a draught... So yeah, Jo why did you send me a text... "Mains."

Yeah, right. Who's Anne? *One helluva Nurse*. Don't look for your reflection in the glass, always look in the mirror....Look at my shoes. I dislike her. BUT then again who is the reincarnation of Bay, a hideous dog, a repellent creature, the runt of the litter! His show name was "Guin". He never got showed. He had a penis, that looked like a pink retractable thing.

"I fingered her, nothing happened, because actually there was no-one there. ''

I could write all day, but not when a computer says "I could write your letter for you." Sinister, isn't it! If you sit in my room, someone will spy on you. There was a chewed pencil in Jo's flat. An HB, vertical black and yellow stripes, but a bit nibbled at the end.

You should care, clothes are important when there's nobody there. Ella, when you apologise to your case worker, when you say sorry, we know something's wrong. You're meant to say "Nothing's wrong." You are everything, and yet, *"Tibet"*. And yet why's she apologising to her case worker, why, we want to know what's wrong wit' you! Are we black, yellow, orange, no we are grey. Give a shit, mate, and? I am everyone and yet.

<u>Nobody, everyone except me.</u>

And then the Jackdaw Strings start playing- *"Only You!"* I sent her an apology, if that's not reason to investigate someone, then what is? You are sorry, there's no reason to be Ella is. Dream on, the title of this book is called "My name", I could never imagine calling it "Sorry". Or anyone's, but her name.

There's a house diagonally opposite my house that's empty. Someone spied on me today! Haha. So yeah, Jo's got my clothes. A Miami hat, she's no *beauty*, but yeah I would, bar...the pink flamingoes. And then, the other day, Blowfish boy from the Casper Sea- my ex boyfriend- drags his sorry little arse into my favourite B-ball ground, Dolphin Square, yeah and smokes like a tumour sitting at a table- proper non-verbal. Yeah, you bitch, she's gay, go away, No\Way! Yeah, too right, no way....And that's how it hangs in Dolphin Square.

We smoke, we don't dance. Ella says it ought to have a roof over it, you know, like made of glass. That's where I met Joe. Boy, is that a short book.

The Hound of the Basketball Court:

It was some kind of blood hunt for curvy E down at Bullshit Creek in Springbok Park, parking her car outside 'Kitcheners'. The day was hot. There was some black guy in a hat with a bobble. I was pirouetting on the *"Cat and Crow"* bridge like a lunatic. He looked up. We both stared at the Oscar'z Road architecture and thought. I laid my head down on the pavement, in the street on the pavement; looked up at the sky and a big black winged bird flew over and spoke of U.R. The *poleece~* came and stung my Britney/Ella's name. I'm going to tear the Voodoo down on Didley Toad Place... Fleece, flesh and wax that's what a good read is made

I collected highly significant feathers

of. *She plays the blue guitar just like a ringin'- a bell.* What's the internet: The Internet is a film. *Shiiit.* Well, let's call it a name...Psychiatry, takes what you're really bad at, at school, and exacerbates it for you. Like charts. In a way that could be a reason, for why I'm not that good looking, I mean, do I have to look like my painting? The drugs I'm on have a name, they are called pine. They (the drugs) take my brain away, and make my family live in a permanent fear of death, or fear of aggression or fear. I know it's a bit of a weird sentence, but the drugs I'm on. KILL. When something's trying to fight death, it does it with aggression.

So, yeah, babe, you're violent. Get the hell out!

The Birds:

I collected highly significant feathers. And "God, said, go back to who you were when you were twenty six." I don't know how things happen, or where I put things, because I've been raped. And in this country, rape fields are yellow. It's a rather unfortunate thing to call, a field, when it's yellow? I used to put my right index finger in my mouth, as a child, and something's happened to my left. I believe, psychiatry made my finger deceitful! The drugs must have affected some part of my brain.

I have a Dr living in my head, but I'm a good nurse.

I'm... It's hard to say, but ...The problem is who, becomes a where, and I'm terrified I'll never go to U.R City.

They ended my beginning:

So I wrote a whole episode about Englenike. Because I saw every because I could of: There was an *"And"* and a *"Yeah right"*, coming out of a drugstore. Yeah, except they were people...Who are you to say I can't come in buy nail varnish, and plonk it down on the surface and buy it before the guy in the queue-in the pharmacy-gesticulates at me!? With his hands sort of like round my face! Really angrily. There was a rather indecisive moment when I smoked a roll-up that previously I'd rolled on the whatever- bus; that was. And I smoked it on gravel under a tree, or rather a branch in Englenike. Then I saw a black silhouette of a man in the distance, and he made me want to stop smoking. I mean, I thought to myself "Give it up, hopefully"...I entered a pharmacy, couldn't find a toothbrush, then went to the bank. Saw a woman in a gold top look at the sun.

I feel I maybe need to buy some sunglasses in Lyndon. Get my nails done, maybe. Felt like I told the shoppers in Englenike,-"What's a mirror? It's ye'r brain!"

The bank, was a bit overwrought... It was a boring sardonic woman called, "KumRun" *Woh-* in a way, her name was not funny, I was trying to get some money out.

So, yeah what's strangers, people who read my book. And then I realised, "Oh God, mum-let's call Paul Goldsworthy, the sun." On account of the sun being bright yellow.

I understood that I am a bit of a traitor, when I walk past the Martineo magazine store, I grin inside, and out, and think "Yeah, I am." Can you eat a bit of red onion and call it a cigarette? Yeah, I'm a comma, out of the punctuation game- Yeah.

There's some sort of higher power. Yeah. My mum's actually my cousin..now. Yeah.

Some things that happen on the way home: PPBA: ? Give a shit, who's Nightmares-On Wax Fed? No way, it makes me sick the roles I play. Or should that be "rolls". Don't I died- I always wanted to write that on my UltraHip/Compact which is what I decided to call this thing on the Inter-net where you put up photos of yourself. And now I know; that- I hate taking apart acronyms. But I could do it forever.

Right- where's the 'Pendant Kate' pub. I know, do you want to come? There's a prostitute lives next door, I want to take Jo and my ex there..

That was worm valley night, I walked home, Bette fell on her face. And I thought, where's Simon? The cat closed the curtains last night: and that's when I knew "animals" are a disease. What's it like being in an incarceration unit for one animal? I take pine for a reason, when everything has a reason was my favourite phrase. I converted the cat last night it was also the night when someone I barely knew tripped over a brick, after I breathed out. What are animals? F, they're disease. How does it feel to walk with a limp, like me Cleo? They say Ella's hands are limp. I heard it on the grapevine. My cat's outside and I'm wondering what she's looking at...

DRUQS:

dr—u----question "Suzy". I threw the v-sign, thought about my art, some guy that had died down Green Heights. "We're the hum, I like humming-birds." A phrase graffitied on a wall in my neighbourhood.

It's Eno-day!

I can't write because they're writing a book for me. Well, I told Mum, I think grey squirrels should be called Eno's. Why? She replied. Because and I didn't say it, but really I meant to say- I think they look like Velo-Vent. I think I said it, maybe she didn't take it in... Maybe she did?

Man, I saw Caroline Paradis at the bus stop. And there were two men sitting at the middle of the bus. Some old geezer was standing in front, as if he was their boss. It was quite a scene. I wanted to go to Arkio today, are you an artist? What's a *"Negro"*? Backwards is the worst thing in the world for a black/ hearted- bitch like me.

Don't walk down Offshaw Down with a planetarium around your head. And then I walked up saw it was Pineal! Thought shit it's the Arnie-vil horror, nah- a good lookin' man walked past. Okey-Dokey.

And is it really worth it, to mention this, but "Won't stop 'til there's piece of glass in everybody." Yeah, I walked barefoot. Ate a can of sardines, nibbled on some blue cheese, a half of a rotten apple, honey, and lashings of it. In a way, yeah! I found the cure for AID.S. There is no cure for AID.S we all die, these days. "It develops into Aids.." My Dad loved smoking. Isn't it enough, to look for someone who's died, to walk the Earth- when I know I can fly. Don't do crack with Moha, because yeah, maybe the police know..? I had ruined a bit of my book by even mentioning them... This guy Damion knew my name before I met him, I didn't know his, but somehow I had to walk away. Go home; it's hard for a woman. He knew mine, how did he know mine? Who was he sitting next to-an old man, who perhaps, was his friend? Well, it kind-a-looked like it. Man I love Spruce, in there something special happens every day... Actually, today I noticed the Da Mufflo Twins had put a colon on the awning of their shop.

The night was the night, I realised no-one believed in me. I visualised my mum as falling from the sky and.. Because actually the cat started drinking from the tap tonight, I found it revolting and I didn't want to kiss my mother *"Good-Night"* in front of a tap, but that wasn't my first thought... "Actually", was my favourite word at school. Please let me leave Lyndon.. I came to Arkio tonight- and I wanted it to end. *Je trahisse pas mes amis.~J'ai des santé baiser partout* ~. Someone left a packet of dark chocolate "Choco-Leibchen" biscuits on the table. It's funny, but it's also bullying. I came in at 8.30pm, I noticed my door had been fiddled with... it upset me. I came in, and the door was unlocked: but maybe it was a way of telling me something. I'm writing (the captcha in the wry) . *Who's Jewel Pasco?* What's morbid... why are there ropes hanging like bits of string under corrugated plastic sheets that function as a roof at the entrance or exit of the market. No-one ever touches them- they blow in the wind, diagonally, I touched one once, when I was in a very bad mood...

Zelda:

Hey, I'm listening in my room to Eugene McNichol- it's a sad song; but it reminds me of my father. It's kind-a funny, but I hope I meet Ezekiel. It can't kill me, it wants to kill me, it wants to mental thrill me, until I have no body, until I'm in a basement going up to the third floor, and there are two people, one is me. The other is someone else..Both of us are giving fellatio to a man, who won't let us go. It stinks. "It's full of Cannabis"- I can't stand it. God is equality. God keeps on saving me. But in a way, I think God is ridiculous, because I don't want to leave my body behind. I'm writing I know why the colour purple in the caged bird sings.

Why do you leave biscuits for me? Does it matter which type, no. Stalwart, horrible black mess. Everything's a photo in my world..What's disability, it's mental agility----for me, it isn't, I'm not handicapped, but I may be a bit disabled. Yeah, right, I flicked the V sign, at the cleaner, because I am a cleaner too... I put the circle around the sick... and that's when I thought I wanted to know why that guy from Midtown knew my name.

---- Make Free---- and what do they do in mental hospital, no work at all.

Is Wack End, a swastika? You bet, *Welcome* to the kibbutz, Ella, he seemed to say non verbally. You Habit-Squalor star bitch from one eyed disco land. Get in my room and put on my make-up.- Well, in a way that's what God said to me. Yes, it is. It's an unlit candle, my stable mate is the Golden Eagle. *"It ain't a pumpkin.... m8: It's a Swastika"*. I stood at the station on the plat-form, and wondered why all the black-hearted women in my life and some of the men; too, who worked in hospi-tals, because of the pills, I mean what is "Nifon", "pine", "Ozmandis" when one is foreign and you come to a country like Ingle-nook and others underestimate your name.. one may become fascinated by the names of the drugs and try and understand the brand names of the drugs/"*medication*" one must "give" to the patients. Once I had a couple of nurses, their names were OLa, Leeth, and one I can't remember because I may have covered it up with memories.

In fact, I felt like I released her name into the air around Habitat Rd. And I did. Her name was Lucia.. and she was my nurse at one stage.

The Neverlution will not be 'Ere Lived.

Q) See Lightning Bolt boy in the Chateau du Gratin Gardens.

A) You leave them lit. I blow them out, here you have a choice.

It's make some noise Day in Ingle-nook. Yeah- _Rool_ this place. Who's a "Siberite", said the skater to the tourist, who was parking a car at the concentration camp? Why it's Ella MAKE FREE. What's Frei/ Freedom- but then I wanted to say "Die". But actually that wasn't true. What are builders, if they're not ODD JOB men, who's the Chinasee-Dragon--- why me, you effin' pink ruff wearing monopods from one land under uniform. What's FUN? Backwards, it's unfunky.

Who lights the fire, I light your fire. You light mine, we light no-one's.

I want to voyage... I read this back to myself and I heard it in a voice. Imperial Weather and Ire play together. You'll never be famous, Ella- so inside I think I'm disabled.

-You don't want to tell a psychiatrist that he'll find out. How do you think that makes someone like me feel? Well. No, it makes me sick when I'm a genius, Robert's a savant.

And actually, pass the soap. Robertttt's a genius. "You back off when that boy gets going…" Inglenook's trying to take my exclamation mark away from me. I'm a savant.

Pass the soap.

Welcome to the Stiflers

Yeah- you can't bring your mother here, who do you think we are? You're going to Strattenlang, Ella. It's a bit scary for a girl like me with a liberty Ticket from Ingle-nook. *Present Tense:* They want to get rid of me, even my mother does. They're pushing me. They ask too much of the mad. What's an unlit wick, it's a candle that's left unlit? Man, I hate where my studio is. I leave the door open. My mum, thinks I'm a complete flop. Just *"loik"* my father, I ought to be sectioned, they can't, they won't.

Do I have friends? Yes, Moira, Alex, Go and Will. I also have a death complex. I'm dying. What's that baby doing, it's signifying it's crying. Because- maybe, it's being touched. But in a way, it's not…And I wrote it when I was quite acutely unwell, for lack of energy does make the heart bleed for crack with Moha. What's that dog doing, it barked, maybe to respond to the baby crying, but maybe it doesn't give a shit. But maybe it annunciated to pierce the air, to add to the cacophony of sounds- the baby crying, the dog barking, because actually when a baby cries, it doesn't know it's crying. Which makes a baby very reasonable, I think. What are reasons, they're natural. Drugs aren't natural. What are drugs, reasons to numb pain, that nature didn't give you that there was a reason for everything. "There are patterns in nature." ask me, "What are patterns?" And I'll say "Reasons". Dogs see in black and white. My real name is Immanuel Kan't Piss. (Itch-R-Us Project). Thanks 'DRUI', you make me piss, hardly at all, I hold it in. But even if I didn't hold it in, it wouldn't matter because I still take the 'DRUI'.

When someone thinks about you, they know they are thinking about them, and you. When I think about someone, I know that they know that I'm thinking about that person. I'm on Dopamine-Re-Uptake-Inhibitors for a reason- But what's dope, a drug I need for energy. "A-sort- a- responsive" unit.

I take crack with someone every day. My friends know I'm on drugs, and in a way it isolates me. Because they know I'm not thinking about them. I'm thinking, but only about myself. I circle the sick, is a way of saying I am outside the evacuees, and I usher them in, to a safe space. "For Ella is the maddest", who will take drugs with Ella- no one, only bastards. And in a way that makes me an angel for the bad-hearted men. Who will take drugs with them, they are dark. Only a woman like me would.

We put her on pine, because she doesn't know what she means- what's *Girdle* when it's a *Broach*? "Yeah, she does a good impersonation of everything my daughter was." You only get one chance, with your friends Ella! I wear Simon's mask to bed.

In some ways I am a Christian.

I've been in a coma, all my life, until I met you-Dr's. Yeah that's right.

"It sounds like a good time to eat/You what?/ He pushed up his silk shirt, looked at me, it was always blue/ Spaghetti's hard to swallow/ Hello Dr W—you look like a dog."

Nothing's perfect, but everything is to me. I can't be a photo for you all the time. I'm sorry, I'm suspended in amber. Yes, it does get a bit annoying, "It's 8.30, because the film's at 9." That was Thali's only sentence in my book. It's not a good idea to write the context in the context, why can't you fuck your psychiatrist? Because that would be breaking the Hippocratic-

"Sometimes, when it's overcooked, it tastes of nothing at all."- My mother.

Hi, I'm a black woman but actually, I'm a twelve year old man, I have my mother's eyes, we have the same feet. Well, when we are sequestered in Tallahasee, there's only Paul to look at. It's the police for my mother, that's the problem.-**SECRETLY, IN A WAY, NO.**-Ella's psychiatric *Chlart*. I walked in without my glasses- and then I realised that she had to touch her mouth when she wanted to speak to me. Psychiatrists's can't have sex with their patients because they are in love with them. I think if psychiatry were to be successful it would really have to examine people's shit...

Psychiatry taught me to laugh at a lie, so I give the game away every time.

"People touch their pockets, when I stand there, and I think they're taking money out, to put in my bucket, or at least I did today and it was threatening, wearing a yellow sash outside St Peter's church." That's what a friend said. Psychiatry happens to everybody, it is a mental health problem itself. What's a cat doing in a house like this? It's a walker, it's incest itself, it's human, it's female, it paints its fur.

I'm a scaffolder and_AIDS on acid to look at.

About 5 p.m

"Thanks babes, see you soon." Ella, it's like other people are listening to you, all the time. I think I offended someone last night? For some reason, Jo, picked me up on it. _Oh, sorry, I should keep the pain still..._ There are things I don't like about your face, it's rigidity...It's facial plasticity...Do a three monther- We can all fly, please refer to the above. Psychiatrists think smoking will make their patients better, for example...

There are frequent cigarette breaks, time tabled into the schedule of the activities of the day in hospital. About every two hours, or if a nurse is asked it can be nearly every twenty minutes. There are shower rooms, but that depends on the architecture of each particular hospital. Sometimes we can use the men's shower rooms...If necessary, when required by somebody when one wants to exit or enter the _Rape_, one has to press a green button, with no sign above it. It doesn't let one know which direction to push or pull the door. Sometimes they can be automatic.

"I'm in Poseidon, it's 1965. Wait until you hear my voice on the phone, mum... keep it down Dr's always watching... yeah they're giving me cupies, soliumanganese, no, not Vax, something called Lbowgrez, and a Sofifone, 100mg to get to sleep. Helen, the girl in the bed next to me, killed herself yesterday, yesterday we had a funeral for her.."

She used to wear a red flannel dressing gown. Toweling, I think. I wish we'd never had Dr Logie round. Mum, he was *Austripe*.

The food's disgusting, all the nurses are prettier than me. They're mostly Upperdex.

NO. Where do you get your body language from? From a Dr.

I sat in a white room, with a Dr, in front of me, and a piece of spinach fell out of my mouth into the glass of water that he gave me to take some pills with. After that I was taken to The Big Mentally Ill hospital. I call Hospital-"Ho's-spittle" because I don't spit, I see things...

What's a Dr, when I know I should be teaching Literature of Ingle-nook, probably at a university, wearing better clothes, knee high boots, and making a living.

What's mentally ill? It's when you can't keep still, for fear of urinating all over the christmas-table. Actually, I'm on pine. Pine's my tranq. What's your favourite film? Ella sitting under the traffic at Yule in a laboratory being raped by her sister, repeatedly, all the time. Non-stop. How do you cross the road after that, without goose stepping through the traffic- well it matters who you play music coming from a radio next to doesn't;-*it*? What is the Interweb, it's for looking up people's mental health problems, repeatedly, again and again non-stop... It feels better writing "people's mental health etc" than writing "I have an etc"...

I always wanted to get with my Dad's druggie friends from Alcoanon.. I had a problem.

<u>Losing Mary.</u>

And then I forgot what I was supposed to say because I was looking at your eyes...I was the family's little problem child, no, Skid Row, actually. How's my dada, the best blast of mother fuckin' sitting next to Margaret in Endslieh, when I live in Sorrel. In a way, that makes a lot of sense, although it's not really right. Please refer to what is going on with that poster on Mikle/Cleaves Road. And what is going on with that poster on Mikle/Cleaves Road? Don't worry I'll do some research. I circle the sick- I polish up the insane. Put some eye polish on, yeah, I heard that once before, once somewhere.

I'm listening to "Mawkishmain" speeded up on the record player. Yes, I'm looking for meaning in a record. Tell that to the Dr. Ella started art school after institutionalisation.

Takes a little time for the dead to make decisions too. For what are the unborn? Ill.

What is a life you once stole- my brother's ? But someone gave it back. Ella did. Actually, it was Sian. Yeah, I had sex with an autistic guy it was awful. Actually, it was only awful because we used no condom. He was called Toni.

The Lo.

I've got a case of the bloody Nora's now...The Brownlo'. Y?

"Je traduis des poèmes dans un hôpital psychiatrique pour des"-problematic individuals who look at glasses like they're disgusting! You don't know how many double visions I've had, mum. What's that day, again? It's the day, you take your pine, again and again and. It's hard to understand yourself when friends think completely. Kain's a fighter, I'm ill, G's my friend. In the

ends, in a matter of words I - **Don't risk it for a biscuit, Rexy.**

All the pretty parcels, I awoke, a brown, broken-necklace of blond-ed hair, *Dred*-ed too. I took cocaine last night. Money has more to give, doesn't it, than offal and codswallop and all that jazzes isn't Brown. You on the brown Oll? Strong Street the massacre. There's a right in every woman's life to see because the blind can see it is their right not to! I have an Oath and that is God's swear that my body remains safe on this place called Hell. Ever seen a woman walk upside down, that was Dina in Northster a black carbuncle in this nest of things that woke me once, from a dream I once had into another dream...

The Coachman's bar red 'n' green.

Somewhere; "Over The Rainbow":- A young woman walks into a pub on a main street. She comes in, pulls up a chair at the bar, "Ooh. Look someone's drinking there" a man says; so he move's his mate's pint. She says "Really? Sorry." The bint-barmaid with more make-up on that a half-plastered cow sidles up to the 'Gal' who now, has found a side-end of the bar to sit at. "What would you like?" says the barmaid, "I don't know, I haven't made my mind up yet," replies the 'Gal'. " You're not getting served in here" "I haven't drunk today. I haven't drunk for four weeks" says the 'Gal'. "You look like you've had enough to drink." And the 'Gal' says "So do you!" The barmaid moves away towards the toilets. And the "Gal" says, across the bar. "I'm on a Tension-Subject- Order," she pauses, "I get given an injection. Of *anti-psychotics*; it's to protect me from people like you". And you're not supposed to have a good time, you're not supposed to drink *"beverages of the alcoholic type"* when you get given ANTi p SYcHotiCs." Maybe I'm known around that area, but-Man! You do not enforce some CRAP onto me when I come in...

"All the trees speak of Everestina." God, great band! Nix that. *"J'ai une urgence partout."*

Part Zero: Extreme necessity to write this down:

Once there was. Man, DOWN WITH Englenike. I BLEED. Because something leaked inside me once. Once there was...That light bulb will never pop-and so we return to a leaking tap, and getting up to change the C.D. "Don't worry, Anne I'll do it." In under one second I'll be there back in the morbid reality. So: Suzy's gay... "Get out! No-way."

Listening to GG on the one's and two's: and in a way that's leprosy but then again who knows where the time *"blo's"* ? I like him. Yeap. Yeepyeep. Cackle cackle. ..oh Tumbleweed me no, The Loe's sang one didn't they. Love- Which is why : 'They get the DOOR." Such is their hate.

I love you, you Cartesian. I've never~melt~.I've never met. Love: poem to a bright boy. You "fuck up"/ You black bastard gone blue...ain't that the truth, Red Ruth/Lover I am. *"Not-there behind the wheel."* The external sounds are so loud. And then I could sing...five days before my birthday. It's not about you or me?

It's about a CRIPPLE BOY'S CREEP CHILD following you down the tripper's daughter. Water's

mortar. Tripper's torture. Quince! And the sun sang..
the "SUN"-"song", don't quince up my tart.

Dirty Looks

Basically you're going to the Paycross for some off-
colour, and that's where the 'Lingo' began. Bloomberg's
showing, mum. Her wig. Next time, you will bring
nothing but you're milky, milky moo man. There was
a point when I cried-"I am the Denial of my father's
self-belief" and a white male said –"Yeah" slightly
derisively- And from that point on; I took the piss with
my body. On 10.Street down by the crossings, oh there
are many crossings here! And a little cranky woman
drove past. I sang out. Below the Cross Father is
"Yo-ho-ho'ing"- with his vanity cap on and a tinkler
the size of a whale. I wrote the lyrics to *Just Saw God*,
on a leper's-daughter soaked in tears not Cartesians.
Orange card me not; for I went past the Charnel and
spoke my name via the guise of fingers to a black coat.
A syringe for this Lamb! They have defiled my body.
I brought an unreal cap from fiver Island, mum it costs.
It costs more or much, much less than 12.50 of
"unwaged payment" into the Paycross Gallery to see
Millicent's painting. Dad entered my soul on the day he
died/lost his body to...He thinks I'm mad but **'of a good
time doin' it'**. So Father Christmas resides. Why look at
your stupid oblong body and say the word costs for a
sallow man:- walked past and he wanted me to admire
him! Or was it just that we 'we could thrash things out'
a bit. Foi Gras. I live in an occupied T.S.O unit for the
back wards. For the poor, bent bitches are bastards to

y'ER. Worse than D'eath's Roar. Tick-tock the miming goes on... topple down.

November now...Flicking the bird, and Oliver said: 'I'm not mad at all,' I'm a total rebel yell as I wear my Kandjinsky coloured coat through the streets of Lyndon: I want you *soo* hard. I could not see to write these words down but.Outside the boyz~ sound like Spaniels?! My body's falling apart. You go back in-you *Mother's daughter,* you sly child of a grandmother named Dolly. Who worked in Farell's Books once."*Wot~iz' wrong*" with you? Is what is wrong with the w-w-world.

And I forgot I was wearing my contact lenses all the time. When the ship went down the ship really did go down. Black Miranda's with soft hair and pale white boys with genitalia! **When i see you** fall out of this shit shop----mental hospital---- with eyes that bre-e-e-d the speed ! That grows like honey from a monstrosity. They gave me nothing there nothing; but crumb and red or white or pieces of med and who are you Nig-ee-la? And who are you necrophile? That's a- Hematite. And failure did not shit that one out for you. Because Lyndon man you-y'u, OWE me a livin' from colour that stains Maps with its *syringe.* And wow Ella! And if you come in one more.. And all their names mean something back-wards 'mere sneezes' **but they are rife.** RIVETT street and 'Up' St. Up yours for my body is a taxidermy/ the tap started dripping... I flicked the bird once. Or is?... 2 "flip the bird"..and 'I am famous.'~

<u>At Home:</u>

Yeah, part Zero mate. Corporation's Station Radio 8... there's some Rock Star from the *'Open Air'* saying

Communion and he dyed his hair. And yeah, Simon on the slide guitar and the Sublets and that's the evidence: On a syringed-inoculation M8! And yeah, some weird man in a-Trojan-militant wedding ring~ 7:23pm. And they sound like 'Blue Pumpkin' gone wrong in/I can't feel a straw the radio just interjected.

It has GH carved in the Luddite's meeting house and give a damn because I feel GUILT, yeah GILT take the U out... and put U.H.T in. I'm going to be O.K ? Yeah, and had I said that before two minutes ago I would have been SECTION.E.D. And that's just a way to kill someone-slam them back in and prove Death through my **_LIFE_**. Prove Death exists by pumping her. Full of excrescence – Marianne just burst a syringe inside me. Latrine2:- it says over there.

Victims 19/10/2093-I AM A PSYCHOPATHIC MURDERER>

Trace's Spelling's is shit. "This lonesome hollow goes on at the Canal."

I went along the radio with my digit sticking out... Or was it my antennae?

When I cross the road I cross:-*Yesterday* Dr "X.." and Ana (Nurse Ana) had a party in my head. They took the cynicism out of me and replaced it with something much more residual. I forgot the Magazine. In more ways than one it seems. I drank resPire through an apex glass and suffered "The thing we don't put words too". On a continual basis... Where is my writing: is it in the feminist publication... Stupid cow who said my camera was a creepy thing and then got her friends to confiscate clammily. And bitchily and Post

Socially-derivatively my camera; and foist upon me the threat of crime as the two girls who had not come of womanhood yet-, were ordered to secure the deletion of an Aspidistra Flying's hooded features. **Just 'F- Off –'*Jollies*.'**

I know what's wrong! I'm being too final, contemplative today; a man asked me for a lighter. It was blue, and he was all-right...(It's sunny or it has been, sometimes I see stars at night and then sometimes I don't.)

For I was the "Sunshine" model at the conference and no-one else:-

Yes, having displayed two goods:-One oil and the other acrylic at the Academy of Lamentation.

<u>Poem.</u>

It was an Image and a half even if..we didn't mean it, we didn't mean it- really- but how did we mean it? & that refers to a look. *One that is not set in stone.* So I practiced yoga and wrote a book. Isn't that enough? It was an image. It was an image looking at the sky and pointing my bird up at *It*.

Sitting in the dung heap while looking at the stars... "BLACKLIVES SORRY". They were my pleas. To say Ellen was beautiful, I had "a mental health problem". Sorry about the spots, the social forbearance- the moments of relief...the five guys...the-

Women weave, men stone. Women stone/men weave. And by the way; Dr Z had always played a role in my portraiture-*drawings*-please. Please refer to my credibility.

...It's just a shit way of saying you're ugly. A MARZIPAN PIG- I'm in Stokefowl Park; irrelevancies of relevancies...The ugh/lies, the inconvenient truse!

A case of the "ugly's", I'm afraid. When. I stand at the traffic lights I look like a Normal. Ella's not normal, she's schizophrenic- Untruths: *Satiny untruths*. Thanks Georges for dying your hair blonde and having some sort of consequence, set of sequential happenings to your life...As in- *La Mort*. I mean, I'm sorry yeah- butt. Ooh! Look a clandestine fag-butt I can pick up and re-roll occasionally/ hesitantly and then again...Yum-yum. And **'FOOLS'** 'ave some sort of control over you're offspring really Wryly, Sirius is a Star. No fucking way, Jossie. There is no rhyme or reason it is you not eye. Tell a lie, let's pry. A strange, obscure man is sitting beside me in this park of all parks ..YOU A-HA'VE~ NO EVIDENCE. And I'm not willing to validate that by looking at you..."I think I don't look... So therefore everything I perceive I do nonchalantly. And blindly, because I have no inner vision: I have no perception.. where as my Inner -*inner*vision is rich and dark/ and my outer perception is shallow and dismal." Unlike the reality that surrounds us. And, *'wot'* you think that's permanent? Down by law..?'

Yeah, and do u know what Anxiety is ? It's a way of-it's a way of not finishing your sentence and getting angr 'ee' with yourself because she's hot. The me in you not, I but ME. It's all about jealousy, apple-yards and waiting for y'er dog.

The Tallest man in The World

Hip city. It is two people in love. White trainer slut jock. E

Roller blade the back street'z.. good blades scrape my eyeliner off, squeeze these breasts Mistress. Eliminate to extrapolate the B's. "Brown Bessie was her name. Mein Lay. My Qwerty, your 'ouz. VERBOTTEN. And *nite time* is right woman of her dreamz. Sleep well 'Bess. "T for Time". My squeez." Tall gourds *gro'* high in Hi-Field. Garth was his name actually. Big slack, slick Guy. Bang on the door. Whorez. *'Ere we go the Ithmus, la chattel.'* chattel whore: Go on dear squaw! Trying to get a habit of writing every day; scribble, scribble. 'Gotta' go to the opticians and a 'Yoga Class'. Also to Caitlin St for an Adult Ed...ucation course in drawing an:-Orange, Ad Nauseam; I remember.

Sifar

I remember a cafe decorated called 'Dolphins & The Sea': turquoise, a sort of Sea- green and snow-white it scared me! Overbearing; perhaps it was? But at the time it didn't matter how I reacted to the fear- I was accompanied by my father. And *brother*, I was a young girl. Contact lenses would help me and to chop my curls too precious they're to.. Today the bin-men came: I was paralysed last night a sudden shower cut the Stillness and someone expressed their wonder at it. Y'onder my window:- Things happen.. I awoke cheerful: 'A red cerise crop-top and black trousers I wore, silver wigs and red lipsticks we wore and so to dance like crazy dancers. Yesterday I was able to write two sentences more or less. Today I feel unequipped. "What's that load of Autistic best- sellers doing on the shelf, un-published!" And then I thought, better get this sent to Stu. After all.. So I humoured myself with thoughts of languishing virulently in this one armed spy hole called *"Mi Casa."* What would I do with myself this evening? Hmm. And I questioned and I pondered and...miraculously, a thought occurred, and it was: Where, what, if and how did I get this far into writing such a book as writing this book.. 'The Bible~Backwards.'.? & for all those out there in the rain, the snow the brutal vagrancies of life as we know it on Earth who want to get shot of this. Keep reading.

Today was blasphemously bad. And it has been bad for a few days as I juggle my thoughts and pass the day. Nearly two weeks have passed since the meeting when I didn't get the magazine out and bullet-proof shock 'em all dead. It was on the 13th of October. I write to mine the dirt that sighs the percolating life of Wryly, *#siriusly,~Sirius is a star* and I am sitting defiled waiting for the shit to hit the fan.

"Chapter One":

In Mohanian's a chazza shop all profits go. They sell skins, leather and silks, topiary hoses, ointments, veneers, shoes and ink in rows and grids. *Leathery*...I buy, I buy a cough, cough **Social Reality Cheque** in there every day. Today I feel blissed out and tired. Red dress lays ruffled on a staircase somewhere East of Englenike. There are 12,million of us! Every life an untold brag! Swear down it is Simon the man of my life. Nameless bu~*sterd*. Or is it, indeed, the man from the National? An American "trophy boi~" for a Venutian such as me? In Nutley Arms there is a massive mirror, I buckle danced twice.. My arms became long lapels of skin. Softly I went slipping- tiredly if rambunctiously on the sly with some cute guy from a social promenade. Oh my leper. This is getting Surrealistic!

Columbine and other authors of their own fates... wreathe and creep over tiles and ornaments. The hospital reeks of urbanity, my quiff feels stiff with hairspray and other product. Unbeknownst we keen and cry for <u>pine</u>. Pine does great damage to the serendipitous aspect of life. Acting on instinct made fetid by ample amounts of totalitarian control. It's dark, I'm in a low-lit flat smoking. I've been in worse places, after all this is my home. *Keenloch* beckons perhaps a trip-out. I'm stuck in Kinzie St. I'm in the park, here, right now, right 'ere. Every cloud has a silver lining or so the bin saying goes. Kinzie-St-park always suggests I change: 'Ave a good time, leave dark things behind. Indulge zo 2 speak in *Sprechen sie Deutsch? I'm so lonely*. I mean, like Todd tried. Am I turning into a mute? I write as a means of survival.

I want tears to flow. I want me mam. I'm soo lonesome. Drew B today, took the energy right out of me, *zo 2 speak*. What iz Kinzie? Where *Iz* Kinzie?

It's dark, it's dusky. Men hate me, women look. Or is it the other way around. So blind, so daft I couldn't *zee* the sunset. Like cotton balls dipped in carmine and rinsed. Foggy blue and orange so gold you could sell it. Clouds turn to pink, defamating as time sinks into their fleshy mass. Hunks of humanity walk through tugging at machines in hands bent on extrapolation. Half baked-two youngsters play in the playground on a bouncing thing as I type. My computer taps away. Whitegheist sang: "Angels, angels, angels".. as I slipped my codeine. Then the heavens opened. I'm in Zone D Library, South west. It's dark, it's dusky. It's about lunch. There are quite a few people here too. Using the library's facilities. A desk, a lamp, a computer, books... I push my glasses up the bridge of my nose... My cousin will find a way that's for sure. Never knew such a life, so far, as yet, I think.

Apparently according to the letter sent to me from Julian McVil, I'm on psychotropic drugs and that's the second condition that I take my medication. And withstand meetings with Annie, the nurse. The date is the 26/10: How to kill hope, ambition, dreams and fear in one shot.

<u>"The time is...20:48"</u>

Wunderbar. Signed, sealed and partially delivered that's where I stand with cult and ethics. Man, I wonder if Colony's a nice place. Woo, man; U! So I'm playing Guilt FM in my playpen for one person or was it my nondescript Unitarian. *'Here I am'* seems to be the plug. The air that winds is the blood that circulates my eyes. *Meine augen sind nicht Sindy's, ja. Aah biss du, ja Ich bin ein*...one "of Vade's leaves," Mate! God, man tonight they're playing a hula hoop special on big screen in Dolphin Square, my fave B-ball ground. And... so tonight I break the glass. I'm only, simply interested in folk that haven't read "Moon's Jupiter". Rage against that beautiful woman; *yazz Herr Strumpf*. Cain V Colony. Jack knife blues. And she says they, the proverbial public, took the piss of my blue suede thigh hi's. So I cussed them up. Globe trotter's daughter-Water's Chopper. Who won the game? Doesn't seem like Arko can tell, *ja das ist das; Mich*. Then again: Up yours, my hands weren't always like... that.And how

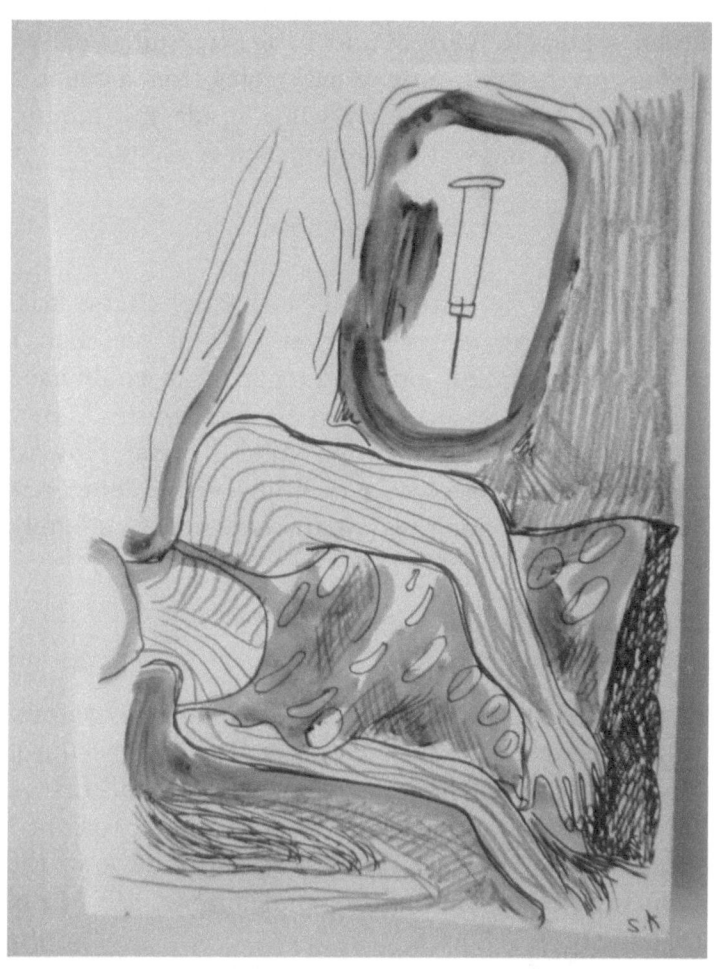

I'm scared

does it feel to be Girl in the Bear Skin Suit! Or is it, in fact DISORDER in North Lyndon, Lightning Bolt-land for the Colony v Cain match, apparently as Guilt FM Radio reported.. Girl in the bare skin suit. Lots of stickers on the lamp-post. What's going from a country when you can come? They came inside my mouth, because. And that was Colony.

27th September.

So Linguo-phone. An Office IT course, of course it is. How inappropriate for a writer such as me. But, I should get a mindless job. Working at Mine would have been. Better, in so many ways. "Strange-ways". But, like things happen. Make my "Mind' a prism. How to progress? Two more weeks then it's over. Volunteer at "C's", that's if I don't get an art retail job. Can barely write.

27/08/200

I want to go to prison give me a crime I can commit. Water's daughter. Offal's daughter. Tuesday the third: You give me time. I hesitated whether to put this first.. I ate an avocado and salad/herb wrap before, tonight I speak to my brother. And then I found out the company's execrable right to condemn me. *"JE M'EN FOU/ I DON'T CARE"*.

God. I suffer. Today the world looked small. I'm scared, I'm scared I'm going to be sectioned in / November. I went to Tracey's Zoo-Trip walk and actually I'm really stressed about Joni lying to me. And extracting money from Thali..It was awful. Had to pay five quid for a pie. Ha ha. Had to pay five quid for a pie because it was heated up. And it was 3.90/40/50 or something. We couldn't, or maybe it's different for Emma because, or *maybe it is,* Emma, because I'm T.S.O'D and on a pine-injection, that, like, I could sort of say my fears to the Zoo-Trip group? And then again, as we waited for that bus, I was standing up and you said... One among many of the rules is that you can't talk about your problems...with the others. And a Zoo-Trip, first the bus. Then the park. And Emma calls it- with wild gesticulation, the "Northster's Park". No, she's not ideal. Man I died in there. Tonight I speak to my brother. The cops are following me but what for? I cannot get a job. And because of that I didn't go to Banquet House Queen. And why don't you work? For a reason. When art's not considered a reason. What is? Money.

I went down to the Swann's it was shut, this being August Tuesday- Holiday weekend. Because in July art doesn't sell well. I felt short without my glasses on and they certainly weren't the same people as yesterday, the day I wore the same dress as today. Which is rather short and shows off my pine-ed and scarred body. Which was once younger. And I'm pissed off and wish I could have stayed in bed but Wil had called. And the woman in the library remembered me and was con- tinental and not very nice and she wasn't very nice this time either. Because when we first met we were not very kind to each other. And my Father and my brother and my mother never hurt me in the way that is done by some people to their children and their friends. But yes, strangers did and do. And I went to Clear Art and nearly got stung after a slight sting in Clear Art, the second being by a wasp, first by a girl. And the women say "Eyes" and the women say "Short". And I talk out loud and after the Swann's- after deciding not to go to Banquet House Queen. I went to Spade Green and somewhat dissed the "Highness" after I cried there in front of a statue of an angel. I can read the future, and it's actually because Ana.. hasn't referred me to a job. And I am concerned about the oral pine, and I ran away from the hospital for a reason, of course! And now you have T.S.O'd me. Which doesn't make sense in order for me to take my medicine so I won't run away from strangers again and- Therefore I probably will be sectioned again? I hope not.

9th September

There's a red cross: when I write. Man, knackered. Six hours on the trot with the East *"End Crazies":* mate. The things I could not say! The survivor's technique: tough, honest, there *were* more attractive women than me there but then after all I am nearly, you know, in my late 30's. So, they did a good job? Then again...what's a strait jacket when you don't wear one? A damned Tension. Subject. Order! Up yours! Read a poem that I think I've lost, wrote it quite breezily, quickly. "Remember me?" The smoker, the vodka carrying "Orange" bottle girl who lied, and yet. My drawing looked good...there were two pigeons there like parents. There's a blue angel in the garden at King's-Hall.

A T.S.O INNERSPATIAL; that's an injection by the way in my wrists and do as Arnie says i.e: Buy a carpet for the flat! And conform to sub-standard regulations and the enormous pressure to not. Years ago I had felt real. I sincerely hope to too. Run/ Rabbit- run. I had looked at my pink rabbit earlier and then I saw a *white* rabbit in a taxidermy shop on Golem's Rd. And the Alice- Poster- in Wunderland from the Chillian'Libs irks me. Strange how things coincide. I desperately want to leave the country. So I spoke the whole story down Requiem Road. It's Banquet House Queen. Simon just walked into the café on Kirk Street, the waitress came over and took our order. Went down Housebound Street, felt I did a non-verbal to a police man at the crossing about a Fun can. Several cars with women of a continent drove past and they hollered at me...I desperately want.

Nippon sun, well, I entered into this lugubrious nightmare a knave. Ever worn a knave before? I had thought I was going to be a teacher. Immediately. All right sweetheart? And then that seemed to calm me down. Do you take sweets from strangers? Unfortunately; I do. Currently, Computer, I thought you had broken. So I'm listening to 'white' noise. Friday: I hope I have a nice normal day. Radio 8 are playing the Steve Filler band, how is that my fault?! I miss Robert. I must do since I think about him. I made an appointment with the doctor yesterday for Tuesday. It scared me shitless to see him! First he drove and stopped at the part where pedestrians cross; beckoned me and looked really sinister. It was outside the Sick's 'Hunter Road' unit, where...

Thursday.

Tell me the truth about love- how I was at Dad's funeral was as I was in The Giant Superstore today where all

the proles disclosed my diagnosis. Perhaps, by infil-
trating my body. But I know that to be a lie because of
what I bore witness to last year. And then I saw *you're*
eyes. At the Doctor's today the receptionist asked me
for what reason was the appointment. I think that goes
against psychiatry and very much for the plaintive: me.
I was happy for brief moments.

"Drive anyone mad going for jaunts to the Lib (s), to
Victoriana's 'The Boot' pub. Act like there's no-one
watching, dance like there's no tomorrow and wear
make-up." A man at the MainMuseum scanned my
computer. Nothing matters anymore. Because what one
touches counts. Such as my body. When **Yes** means No
then **Oui** means.? I heard the worst trap-door sound at
Latent Fields from a car. I went to the contact-lens
centre or should that be Glasses R US, Glass as I once
called it. Saw a hammer by the Mercury in sweet pre-
paration for some actor who played an artist in a film.
Yeah, saw! Grinned at a man on a motorbike. Maybe
it's the way I stoop over this 'set in stone' corpuscle or
should that be otherwise known as a computer?
'Degenerate Art. At *Skool*~deynn.' When I returned
home after visiting my old art school, there was a security guard there upon entering.

'I'm writing the bible-backwards.'. I don't like being
here, I have nothing, very little to do, and Tracey orders
baguettes. Could these people be indications of life
elsewhere? But they are bodies. As am I. Psychiatry is so
violen/T.

I have a hang-up. Saw Nick outside King's Head.
They were all lined up behind computers in the Library.
Saw Simon tonight. I actually had to act like a

supermodel. In a completely fake way to speak to him. Is it because Simon is ugly?

Or am I? I was wearing a beauty spot. I know I'm not as beautiful as Marylinn Munroe. I brought her calendar yesterday. I had to act to see you. Because or else you would have walked away. Earlier at the cinema I thought to-I have lost my black book- buy sweets! Do you really think I'm mad? I ran through the streets of Lyndon and some of it, I'm sorry; if I upset anyone. Siren's everywhere! So I called Thali it has to be kept secret. These are my eyes- this is my body. Why break the T.S.O. Leave Ingle-nook when the Churcher's have stopped chiming. Syringed on August 28th is it? September, October.

X

When you don't do much I see. I see the world for what it really is? I just heard my lap-top bag open. I lost my *evident. "Mardi-Aout."* What's fame all about? Money, dollar and gambling. And act like it. Because it's on the notes of pine. That yeah, if anyone or you have a *'History'* of heavy gambling then don't take pine meds. 22nd October. "Betty with the Good Hair-" has nicked my?! I've put the VC on and then I thought I'm not up "Bitter-honey\ Sympathy" And then I thought, before I left, "I left the door open." Man, I hate Lyndon. And all you Lyndoners dress like you're in a hot country. Because; I'm a fruit! And all of the people behave as though I have halitosis. You're not supposed to hate where you are because if you do...I enter this evening. The world knows you are God's kite flyer. I can't find my book. It had a story so sincere I could not. Last night:-

Really, Diwan. What's gas-lighting..? **I am writing the bible backwards 4 Christianity's a law.** Slight relief. I didn't break the T.S.O or ditch the injection.

It's Socialist day on rat-worm pay. 20th/08/

Flew down a street with an umbrella after purchasing a box of matches. Feeling rather like an idiot: I continued walking and then I started running. I saw Michael Whistle from 'Without' a play on at the Amphitheatre, then I saw a hammer. By a glass vestibule of a Restaurant called 'Mauve's Rising' a restaurant that I had been to. With a boyfriend of mine a few years ago.I felt ashamed. The T.S.O isn't really working, whatever it is...anyway. It is simply an order to be injected. Bleak isn't it? Then, last night in "*Solo* with Don"- was quite amazing, got drunk, in a beige dress I danced the rumba. So, yes, birds fly and I collected their feathers years ago.

'I walk a blind line for them'.

That's when I'm on the road:- I am God's daughter and Adolf saved my life-once. The police saved my Life: (Omit). And then again/ "Throw us an old Copp..ER. U have been abused." I was and have been and currently am abused! I drew the secret... "Actually, total social distraction shall ensue if you write his name "Dr Iz-E-R-A". *I* went to the "Computer, The Eye"...*What I like to call the "plinth"*. A.k.a King Dynamite also known as a big rapper wrote a song about me! "Without you there's no heaven". It is fear that makes me "omit". It is the tramp who looked like Jesus Christ that reflects the desire for such an utter palliative as...what's it called? PSYCHIATRY...actually give it some credit; capitalise it.

Ella you are a kiss. *La plus belle de tout.* And **Dad** soothed me, or that ought to be - sequestered In Talla- as he – once somewhere else... Once was. I walked tonight. Past Alfie, the sun, and the "*Nihilists*" of the World hooted me as they tore past- I had to put my body back. I had to reflect the capacity that w.... And the current President said: 'Ella's life is a gift'. Is this a work of fiction, no but psychiatry is- Because my lungs are rotten like bad-water. Broad Market... why is this..? Crap..? Because we remain in the physical. No... no-one has suffered more than you, only everyone hasn't..As I wrote; I found I was in the 'White Letter Flat.' You can't have a sip.. but you *can have* Marko; Marko Pace was the man who saw my(Angel face) for the first time. 'Herb, or whatever his name was/is who also saw my face and actually my Father saw, it too. Saw my eyes for I did not have eyes to see- At this moment.... "*Il' y a un bon et un mauvais et pour sa. Il y'a un bon et un mauvais.....*"..So to disprove *Psychiatrie.*

What are words if they're not hard graft. What are X's and O's drawn on a Clipboard? My father only abused in my dreams. And Terence- the 'Nurse' smiled. He smiled a Gold-china smile or should that be a cold 'Chinasea' smile with his gold-teeth. I handled the gift... (Ha ha. There is dirt under my nails, I stood on my kitchen table and hulled out my fears)... The Bernese language does not do Justice to:

a) Listening to Radio 8 b) Buying radishes c) Putting c's before D's; 'Before Days'.

The beauty. Uncle Ian has the beauty I gave him. I couldn't write Uncle without you, without feeling ashamed of using the noun "Uncle." As it socially signifies...What I was going to write was utterly euphoric and it was 'Sound'.

"Jesus The Rohypnol Games"... and then The Drawing was consumed. Who is Stu- 'Little alien-that is the "Paint box of colours?" And " 'Cause is it chic, Suzy?" Is it worth recalling? Doesn't that mean I am in danger of defiling my "......" That always represented to me, a book. "I am Mass". I am Time's daughter... Sit in the liminals at 23:12pm...YOU ARE GOD'S ... What is abuse, but. An unfinished sentence in a dwarf ward covering the hand that feeds the child weed in a bedsit .Or in a mansion. Me

– the Doric column, strikes again. Father forgive me. I am the immaculate conception of God's inflection and so be.

The White Letter Flat

"As much as my tweed suit." Clearly. I hesitated as I gazed at the ...... lighter. Rafe Gambaccini eh. These are Lyndon's most disabled girl drawings. I shall protect him. Don't look at me for solidarity... And I knew. With Tali's back-arrow. Back- black- hand-brush she had fisted "Myopia" with so much gauze-and; *"Just as I had fisted The Blow-away Road with..."* Shut up... Pegasuses, the volume of the radio turned itself up.... 'Times- Please and now for all the Solomon's out there Jesus is the Son in all of us. *Gay* as fuck but; what is a backwards door whore?! Jesus is your victim so those that worship at the door are fools of a ... and four-some reason I blasphemed and said "No".

I can make a joke out of everything. Robert, the world is a round shape. I'm concerned I have lost a part of *'le livre'* all the hullabaloo I made in those cars, and yet. Robert you also went to the Dark Side-you are the key to my destiny! I love you so much...I went out after writing and went for a long walk past the War-Memorial in Blossom Park where they... they have the oddest metal entrances?! I surreptitiously told nearly everyone I met the title of my book...as a way perhaps, to avoid Chance. I am convinced she must have defiled Belle. Under no circumstance send her to the secret "Sanitorium for Children". Biscuits at breakfast, lunch and dinner! A mossy swimming pool. Dresses for boys. And coats for the girls such as they are. I picked a feather up, the spit of you saw me in a car and said...'No' or something. Having been so defiled- the comfort of Comfort, Hella, Bosphorus Blake and other shits. I saw free flowers in the City, a yellow rose in a puddle. When someone has no money you help them out. Not ten pounds here and there! I Stasi-ed around Seville Rowe. They're throwing the dichotomy onto me. Went to Hartley's Square. 'And when Robert saw the leader's portrait he scowled. In front of Colonel...' My dad said my mum had sent us to *'An ill place'*- If I don't smoke Simon can hear me. 'She wore a yellow jacket.'

We live in the subliminal. Perfect example of this is "Calendars are days to me." Or rather "I'm worried!" Behind the Bush. Don't bother getting behind the Bush. In Deleuze they *r* children. We emit time: Time is my mother-*"Marilyn" I caught your star"*- You will face divinity like me and see her. Psycho's took ten pages off her face.

The hand in the shit pit was mine- Lilah you leave that girl alone! They planted a wild flower field at the site I..."Shears Guild Bridge". The police were my sheep. Attest your madness. Are words deeds? Words are ... (I don't recall) but in Hartley's Square I saw a Pyromancer there. A week Wheelchair Access: Services;- and Newspeed have not been in contact. One phone-call from me to Anne and a physical entry to the Chowdhury centre to ask Tracey to call me! 14th-20th August. Wednesday 16th of Aug..._

Codeine choice and the Tourettes Man.

Sum of the **merde** I have seen is undeniable. Regrettably the outpouring of bad-ish writing for Don Brasco's short story gift that I sent him online was in actual fact about a spot. Tyronne is prophetic or was. Because he was happy today in the hopes he'd see me. For a modest reason I thought how pathetic he was for hoping he'd see me, is his life that drab? Saw Todd a big fat Gek who feeds me Nescko's Coronation chicken sandwiches when *I am hungry* ! Is it Dear Doctor, I once wrote a book but I lost it. Break The 'Tension. Subject.Order' the week I trifled with that notion, and what's Northster about? Keeping me, obviously. I had my doubts...not *"manger les oeufs. Ne pas me fouetter."* Benediction night I kowtow down the *"rue de Lyndon"*... What's a fish riding a bicycle/ toothpaste kisses/ Doric Columns... Money Mum: She milked ... Three

"Beet on Broadway."

~*"Sum busterd"* shouted Bee-tle-Juice. And then, rather regrettably I ignored a compliment from two women of the Sub-Continent.

Because of a few friends of mine...

It's turning, yeah *It*, is turning a negative into a positive! Or is it, Ell's because I have slagged off ...Penelope... and Tracey... Even though she works for psychiatry. And that's the hairy beast! And that's the double blind, 'You' have a body and a mind and they're not separate. And yet how can your body not be separate from your mind when I'm on a T.S.O? So why are you, doc...making my body mind my body's mind. *Fuckwit* Jo' does not approve. How can one not believe in a mind-body- separation when the mind resides in the body? And then again if we are talking then why are you not talking? And only feeding me meds for my body? (I thought quietly inside that Julia should be the reluctant mistress of. I heard you... stranger: mimic her laughter.)

Alex Hong in Up' St.

"Tongues are for voices
Hands are to speak with."

I wore a swinger. Yes, that is a *Strait-jacket*. And they took it. And I take IT. Because I have Lady up looking at me, a beaut' photo, even now "*Her Image...*" seems to be controlling how I write. The superstition has come back because some things I want to say but I should save them for art! *O art,* how I miss thee! Saw Codeine choice walking up past Englenike Council Buildings. Which reminds me of characters that are so symbolic such as the man in the Englenike-Council jumper outside Simon's house the day of the strangest football match with a mock Justin as referee...

I was *told* and insulted and maybe he was kidding, but Tone, a patient in Northster said I looked like Codeine choice. There she was! Red bandanna sticking out and big glasses on, a wry buck-toothed smile.

Woke up had a roll-up before leaving the house not without the usual torture of thinking about giving up! Every time I walk into a shop and make my order I speak somewhat distortedly as I have a terrible fear of having halitosis- my mother functions as my motivator in some ways; a sounding board to encourage me to do *'busy work'* as my father would have put it. The other night was high Dwyght actually as opposed to dwipe, a case of the Dwipe Card about her. A bad thing too, that means. I let Je-ss-y down I think, jokingly: we had walked up Alderman's Walk and there-*There* is a mock red telephone box. I grabbed the handle and it's glued shut! All illuminated inside. As God's swear should I subsist on cheese and carrots alone?! There were barely any stars in the sky on Sunday the 13th the night I was supposed to contact Robert. I slept with Simon and we kissed, beer fell all over my book.

I still owe H.Sigh fifty pounds and Jess's asking for her backdoor to be paid for, since I lost the keys to it... Surprised she remembered in her purple haze?! Man, I wish I'd got the things from the shop today! Spent so long thinking about-'mental health problem' as a term... I came up with *"cyclothemia"*, or something. I remember reading 'Elucidating the Memento' by Chay RedjamAmy's-son and the*"cyclothemia"* appropriation was given to people I can't name check; artists, authors and poets. Because perhaps I too suffer like them.

Many have suffered but not all of them are in the gutter looking at the stars through one contact lens one hand loose... breaking on the wind while snapping gold fingers in a bar-room-bar in New Rork. So I shit shuffled myself down Lollipop road and snuck down Lytherbird Road tip-top of it past the church, a man with quite unfeasible tourettes was high-diving, skank rippling, and jive talkin' quickly.

Today was mustard. Slept, in and out; of the bed. Roll-up, nectarine, saw Tom of Hardknox Place. We didn't even say hi. Saw Soul Bird. *She has feet the sound of glass.*

<u>Extremely Sinister</u>

In the summer, and actually when the weather's fine children play in Dolphin Square. Some days when I'm there I feel a horrid non-verbal and entirely unsaid feeling that the adults don't want me to be there...On my journey or walks from A to B I see feathers, some black, some white, some downy, some smart and long, some normal, some roughed-up and scuffed. I used to collect these with a goal in view. I hope they have no relevance to 20014's Ten-R-Us Project? I looked up the meaning of O.K after a woman asked if I was O.K. I make bee-lines for these feathers sometimes. Without knowing I cross the road diagonally look down and "Hey!" There's a feather.

Cop C, the white veil, wore a white veil. First made a bee-line for *Beyond The Regard* and purchased it at 3.95. The net covered my face. Suddenly in the crowds, amongst the humans it was nearly as though I couldn't breathe. Simply because they could not see my features... Reminds me somewhat of O.Pendergrast-John's portrait of me with my face in a plastic bag. It should have been orange it should have been from Bayne's. I was thinking prior to that; I'm not marrying Don! The mild 'acting out' and mad thoughts stream of consciousness; occurred along Benzedrine High Street and up to Realist Road in the joonish area of South Lyndon.

Well, you can live with joon's, coke's and Lish's why can't you live with a woman?

What? Is this roll-up supposed to be reality check? *That I'm a poor squaw.*

Last night went to Simon's didn't go in or knock the door. Just stood outside. Thinking of sending him £10 so he can see me then the thought occurred to me of how boring our relationship would be if we started seeing each other again? Woke at 2:15am after waking from a nightmare of sorts. Ate a nectarine, cooked some noodles. Then woke up this morning shrouded in the usual fear of perhaps, not having anything to do. Although yesterday I met Dan who writes and draws but probably_ also has a part-time job. Seeing Don today later at the Florist's, not as if I have the twenty I owe him... or any fags, or any disposable income to spend wildly. *Must* get cv sent to Penelope if not today by tomorrow. Jo's convinced I broke the door, I lost the keys, there's a difference.

There's a man with a leaf blower outside it's really loud and irritating! Can't believe the bouncer from the other night is the same guy who worked at Zone's five years ago.

Wonder how much money I have today.

Saw "Chuck-Dophen," "Flav" and other *Enemies! of Crime* painted on the wall. In Dillard's. Painted in bronze, brown, gold and green. Tasty, I thought. Joe showed it to me, after my sojourn in Dolphin Square 'apologies' to Jon. T for crank calling him to find out who's # it was.

Walking from Armageddon, saw Tom D who's a bit peed-off or something? Cuts all over his face, scarred up. Pretty rancid. Paid him for a cigarette. A 42 pence gone, at least he took the money! Unlike the couple in Saint Peter's who barked- *'There's a shop round the corner'*. Finally made it to a Geko's café and used the Interweb. Robert says he'll call tonight. I've run out of 'phone credit. 1 more trip to the library... Odd: how Tracey and Anne aren't getting in touch... A guy wants me to come see him, telling me down the 'phone how upset he is, sitting at the table talking to himself ! Trying to get answers, crying and drunk. "It's Hell", he says, "Really it is". Sounds just like me!! Wants me to come to Greenwood-Ford today to see him. More into meeting for egg and chips in this restaurant he's saying is good. Can't call him back so better get on-line.

Friday the 18th of August

Had a dream last night I was crying and the tears were true and it was in front of Solong/Services and Simon and I woke and I thought go to Simon's house. *Past the Elma pub et cetera.* Used the Shearer's as a loo. Walked on... Down Habitat Road and saw a feather, a father and his child were walking behind me and I was standing still the father walked straight into me- Heard you're getting away, Simon; Justin told me.

I'm sitting at the John's. Yes the 3 Jay's. Do you actually know what that means? Hate, fear and I just ponced a fag off a cool guy. Feel like the fact that I approached Beatone House and even asked if they sold individual cigarettes incriminates me. I asked in the tobacconist's, of course, but of course. The fact that I'm even writing this somehow is shit because it's made crap by the environment I'm in, do you understand? The 3 Saints. No, I also haven't ordered a drink. And women loathe me. I'm definitely dying my hair blond! Because currently I have no money. 'Looks like a 'nice' person,' and actually as am I, 'Ella, you're an angel.' I have been told. The book is getting somewhat post socially derivative if not identical to everything you ever made. For Ella the world is round meanwhile in a post Dyspraxic world I intend to go to Zoom and study. Write to the University first. I was in 'Cum-Down-Bra', which used to give me nightmares. And O...Dear computer, you spoke to me.

How I lost a boyfriend

So I'm sitting in Dolphin Square and thinking... I really do love you. I have searched with all my heart to think of another. I cannot stand being without you. I feel blood flow inside my skull. People fling it on me all the time- Anxiety. Or un-disco-ordination, (it feels like) and that the disclaimer is: 'You'll probably throw it in the bin'! Could I love you more? I don't know. If it's raining; for today I wear a crown of pain. I'm showing a painting @'Thing's Hall-I love you Simon.

"Je suis un autre maintenant." You've gone on a retreat with your Daddy.

Yes it's funny in a pathetic sort of way. Then again my predicament is awfully sad.

Burst into tears after speaking to Justin who got too close on purpose to insult me...

I can't take the pain...reverse the story. The birds wouldn't let me...

Book the gallery and have a show surely then Simon will see me. 'I like your art, I think you're beautiful' that's what he said on Tuesday the 8th of August! I'll just become a bruise to you. And you to me an axe. Something must be done. Forgive? It's like hitting my head against a brick wall. You obviously don't love me anymore! For being/ sleeping with Anny and Mark Merrion in intervals when we'd split up- anyway. You will find me in another. *"Je suis un autre."* Pay more concern to your fellow passengers in this place called Hell/P. So you've gone on a retreat. You've gone with Jodie (the omphalos) to make what we had all a blur. Ella's ill when that's said in my head by a third person- then an ambulance siren goes off.

I was looking at a feather. *"Wish I'd never met her"* is the whole point of the retreat, isn't it? We sail too close... What do you do when you run out of glue? Find passages stick together in the remembrance that you will be forgotten. So Simon it's over. Yes it's funny but dreadfully bad.

Psychiatry is Police By Proxy.

Cross me out, bastards! *Et Simon a ete assez silencieux.* It is the truth.

And psychiatry wants no cure, it just wants to kill me. And the police act like "Oiks" because *it is against the Lore* to do that however because they're paid to do that: to follow the...Dr's. When I think it ought to be by the police. Because, yeah, what are emotions if they're not? Because what are emotions if they're not yours to have..?

What's yours is not mine to have. You do everything the way you do everything.

The man in Lauder's went behind me, picked up the Slim-line Juice can placed it on the ledge somewhat higher than the bit of the bagging area which/what is still in the bagging area and then I could pay.

Ne pas prendre la medication, et...ils va trouver une raison d'incarceration...Novembre.

It's all the long walks, must be or the walking outside of the Stripper's 'Bar'. Or going to Sousse Gallery or walking down Habitat Road. As I try to find a reason for the fear I'm feeling.I know the lyrics. It wasn't spoken it was seen. Dr Schweppe.

...They thought you were a prozzer, they thought you were...a stripper. The me in you that sees the eye in you; Psychiatry go back to the tree.-"I eat, we're happy.": A horror story. I saw a woman in a stripy dress pull the...air from the air with a spiteful and quick arm gesture. *Those ashen wounds* of my face... the age I'm in, the scars of history, the bike outside, all the things I said and felt ! And ignored the children at the broadway, and ignored the signs of violence and leapt on past the competition and knew what I had seen was true as I barnstormed Lyndon. Because I wanted out.

The Whole Point.

We make social contracts to lie. We lie, about the truth and then we wait for death to validate our lives. Because I stop and start talking on the air: Ella was sensible enough not to say that out loud... Little masturbators. Permanent psychosis until you die because you can't stop until you die, that's a death sentence babe! I'm in love with the purple misanthrope. There was a ruffled cushion- actually an old pillow left on the sofa the time Simon went missing. It seems significant. And then an ice cream van arrived, outside. After I went to knock on your door.. As Rav said 'That's it' there is no alternative to this reality. Recover from what? Social matriculation. 'Yes, I have seen all your trinkets.' When Ivy (Justin's girlfriend) is the only reality and you're a yogic teabag.

Go to dormitory sleep wake the hell out of here. A thousand ships I have flown. Go to Gym. And tennis and swimming. Back of the street, all the time. I fled why the poet why the writing the *Pee* a thousand castles; a million blinking eyes. A cradle, a small mouse or something. My mother, black eyes.. A pout; a lip- a swimming pool. A fraudulent mistress. A winged creature: A broken phone box. All the worried!! Very drunk. A million shiny pieces: "No, I like you."

Smash the pool. I want to die. I want Emma... In my mouth. The cats lie. All the places are crime..I finish eating. "I need a bra." A million wrinkles, Keep talking! A million, thanks. I love it. Sex and Lucille. *Ten out of ten, sex*. Filth, a plastic bag... Don't pretend I'm not here. "What am I doing?" There were ten, ten of us. Then there were nine. *"I desire you."* I make the most of myself. I'll sleep with you. You go... There were ten irritants, fifteen of them! Bleach. Then. Then I asked her to leave! There were fifteen women_ Only eight had left their skirts on... then there were fifteen men and she was **beautiful**. Very happy... Eleven times, they came!! Come in my mouth. Tell me more? Her breasts, her ass, her pussy. Fifteen of them. Eleven out of ten. Fifteen women. And then a mouse.. Write more. Ten people, fifteen of them in my head. Laughter. There were ten of them. Fifteen scarred. All the time. There were eleven. Ten pounds of it. Mother, Burnt King. Only chips and hamburger; there were fifteen. All of them above! Above and inside my head. All of them straight. Sexual fantasy. "You'll be lucky if you get a cigarette. An ant. A small device." Damn Council! I eliminate the book, looks and books! Fridge operator- Lion's Pride...You see; the air? Fifteen to one- go! Draw. It's free. Yeah... Yeah. No bra, no knickers...*No doves*. Go see Tony. Tim Piano. All the rubble. Yeah, nice. Nice isn't she? Absolutely! The voices in the head? That thing. Alan. My husband? I love you. You love me? Why? What have I done babe? Not enough.

The 19th of August

Today, well today. After having spoken to my brother, who rest his soul is a fine upstanding solitary individual with a wide bent for that sole intent: I don't know. Some of what I write is? And then again, the day, the day- today- this weekend promised fine weather. I slept with the windows closed with the Shush theatre on my mind as an application. And if you think, masses of Archdyke road, dear Reverend that my life amounts to a collection of disposed of fags along the pavements when as the '68...Spring slogan in Uropa says, completely famous and oft' quoted *'Beneath the pavement is the sea.'* It is the author's legacy that I take the right to mis-quote and perhaps or so; often. So I harvest the cigarette butts of lonely strangers who discard them. Whose sole intent is to live, like me! Sweet hypocrisy. I miss my father who lives on in my soul. Yesterday the fear was strong and cloying. I told Robert the truth about finding the five pound note after Sr. Winston Epoch had winked at me. From behind a plate of glass, from a poster of fake fivers! Providence, eh! The horizon wastes. Petrarch and Euripides, Sophocles. Friends. Avoiding a man I screw as I don't want to screw him. Brought me gerberas that paled in the moonlight. Here, the flat is safe. Could do with a carpet? But more on that later. In the next episode of Ella's decline and serve. Am I submissive? Dear reader, please infer. The sentences about the five pound note, well this reminds me of what I name the puddles I see, the *vitrines* the pools of rain water that the sky forms on the pavements. The eyes of the angels. Direct communications between the astral (skies) and Earthly plane. 'So go down the canal and fish with a bamboo cane for disease. Like a good one should.' (like "a good angel should..") The Canal where the graffers put the pumpstone up it! Big licks of cocadymol red and white asp'rin blurs. Licks of grey and my hair swept up in a "turn-table" at the fore front of this "Fair_ Ground" I play dice the switch on. For I'm a poor boy today and once I was *'Rage Against The'*...A stone's ticker of histories! Try and concentrate hard enough to love you, you oscillating dichotomy of shit that has entered my blood stream. Where is your father? In me inhale the ghost of a pair with hair that hurt my mother on the number 4 bus to Nowhere's ville. If you think about this literally where the fuck am I going to live is pine helping you in a way, no. I am still hurting myself, my body hurts, arms hurt; Because yeah. **Yeah.** I mean it's only *cigarry*. WTF is cigarry? Psychiatry: it has absolutely no relation to the origins. Latin. Get the fuck out of "Heil's Heaven" Girl. God, just figured out what that means. It's a disgusting rank acid bath full of crap! And men that pick the eyelids off you. Irreversible I think about what... Hash tag 1) Ella you have seen the world before it was lit. "He" reads the book. Piece Mode. Only the future cannot tell what's well. God is the Devil and the Deep blue Sea, Ali ! Ali Lacan. Currently I am enslaved stuck in peace mode by the Icthmus. Aribindo... Yogic Expression. What would happen if I left the section I'm on? What's well about you? Road Island shooting star. *Noiseuse:* Hash tag 2) And because I am living in total fear of being killed- hurt- sectioned, thought, needed by myself and others and R and 'Belle' and there it's gone again. So WTF are you-police- playing at thought? A thought just re- appeared again: WTF are you playing at "killing me softly" to somehow abstain/ abscond your suspicions that I am evil. 'I have murdered people.' Now at – whatever time-totally absolved of this. Why? Because of the time and the fact that it's a total lie. Schizo- and to be soiled permanently... Permanently unhappy too; that I am somehow ill, mad, sick, psychotic, yep, or claim I (you are anything because you are nothing). 'I've killed loads of them. Put that on the Remedial or *I'm an idiot;* and because I decoded that- I have a mental health problem. After I die I will look upon myself that they were blind (!). Hooray. I mean WTF is that ugly bitch psycho rapist murderer executioner penniless president father-fucker dangerous-weirdo doing? Why can't she be her and we be it. Gravity has a way of taking things, no pine my *murderer* has a way of taking things! I walked about. I walked also; with my arse hangin' out. 'I'm not on drugs, officer.' Well, at least not naughty one(s)...

Yesterday. 'I walk a blind line for them.' Two Joon's walking out of Joonsbury's. Sunday was mental. Actually, hadn't slept for all of Saturday: Went on this mad manic walk all over Lyndon. Did a window shop down Bolton Avenue, walked down the 'Circuits' past the Academy of Arts. Marylinn's a blonde, right? Thinking about dyeing...there I got the answer, dye it blonde again, babe. Late night Lyndon got scared though! Been mistook for a *prozzer* before? Not by coppers. And then in Orb's, early Sunday morning felt lost!The *feathers~* everywhere. Found some matches walking up Pondarosa Road where the Deaf/Blind are. I walk a blind line for 'em and that's at the traffic lights on the white painted pavement squares. Ended up in Blaudendale opposite Hayling Fields. Oedipus...and the **"Ass saw the Angel", that's from the Numbers book of the Bible".** I'm an angel, man. According to the computers they put pennies and feathers down on the street when no-one's lookin'. I'm not collecting feathers if it implies I'm a criminal. Saw a real-livin' saint outside Cewo's School Form College. Do saints linger and have anything to do with Cewos? Finally slept.

Awoke and felt 'normal' I had cracked open so many theories about being mad, proved them. Called mum burst into crying in Cewo's. Spoke to Tracey she was rather terse, short that is. Now I'm home, the flat looked great as I entered, ate my Massifburger. Went to Rory's brought some shoes from a shop along the High Street; blue, lacey. Black leather... my black- leather-trousers from Mohanian's have scuff marks on them. Saw some feathers; managed not to pick any up. Saw my Soul bird yesterday eating chocolate from its wrapper. Snigger at no Other for I am 1_ 2. Went to Dollar and brought... Brought forty seven quid's worth of things I needed. Food too. Still need washing powder though. *Buy it:* Curtain rail, frame, bookshelves.

I am God's kite-flyer And I said; *"What she looks like standing at that window,* as if wishing for some Apocalypse! There are no reasonable explanations... Yeah, Ella took it. The victim in the family. And she; my mother looks at her smart phone. *It'll never be published.* There are too many people digging with picks by the side. I'm a slave Mom. I've never been mad. I'm starting to find out what I am to this family. How dare she mention Simon. *"That man."* Because Ella was in love! Because people are brainwashed to *death.* I think it's good to maintain(...) that I'm not mad.

I don't want this woman to come round. But in the end it amounts to everything and nothing! I remember me sitting right in front of her being told off by her: *Carpet, carpet, carpet.* Got to get the carpet (*what a stupid word*)- in. I fear I'm endlessly on the edge of having myself sectioned, imprisoned and drugged... Am I a weirdo? I don't want her to see my things, to see how I live! I don't want her in here! Because I fear she judges me! She criticises me, she judges me along lines I do not know. I understand it's all part of her job, perhaps it's not? Perhaps it's personal I very much doubt that. To smell the apartment, to drink from my mug...to see the things I love. I don't want her here because she can section me or... Based on what? To know how I am in my own head space and make judgements on if I should change later. To set me in stone! Times twenty-six sculptors of statues.

In the hospital.

There's Peter makes me swallow my pills. Makes me stand. The dirty injection girl. Makes me open my mouth... He looks down my throat. Makes me stick my tongue out. Makes me take all the water; then makes me sit with the others.

It's hard to write down abuse isn't it? There is a man, first he greets me there's a nurse forces me to swallow my pills- Forces me to stand- Forces me to look in his eyes:-

He looks down my throat, forces me to stick my tongue out, forces me to look in his eyes; he sticks his tongue out. Forces me to take all the water. All the water; makes me sit with the others. *Ivi*'s room now. It's hard to write down abuse in a ward of "Hospital" and hospital's. Theirs is a man, first he greets me... There's a nurse forces me to swallow my pills. Forces me to stand, forces me to look in his eyes. He looks down my throat, forces me to stick my tongue out, he sticks his tongue out. Asks me to lean my neck back. Forces me to look in his eyes and he sticks his tongue out. Forces me to *take all the water, all the water*. Makes me sit with the others while he medicates the others.

There's a way...out?

Walkin' right towards me, dark and imperial comes a black man, I know him from somewhere... He calls it the "Eye-Opener"...the truth teller ; later I would know...he assured me. Come on. We sucked it from a blue tube, and the roses glittered in the dark night with their moon-bathed eyes. He says, "Inhale, hold it in, *I do*". Then we lay on the grass, of an estate. Maybe; there were people watching? A fat man walks past us, we're looking for a phone box to call to: "Get some more" ! I see him, Moha says "You wanna fuck him?" I think to myself; *I think* I could make some money.

The hostel's on Braulein Road. We have sex there, and I seal the feeling in with roll-ups. Then love comes in: Pumps through me-except it's 2025! And it's two years since I first felt *"Love"*. I feel the exact same feeling, two years later.

Now, I think it's because my heart is broken, the crack somehow *"Revealed Love"*. Simon used to give me notebooks except now, it's Moha giving me an Erskine silver -embossed notebook. I don't know what brand it is? I threw it away.

He walks me to Fastbury , the sun's shining and he asks me for a fiver. I give him three pounds in coins, he gives me a penny back. Moha has a gold tooth and a red-left eye, but boy; was he hot. Not before mistaking an eyeliner pencil for a pen! Because I ratify the world-Because I'm not impressed by a magician from Sifar.

They put plasters on tears

For I have seen the light, the light that shines inside men.

The light that pours from Xyra's eyes on the Pacific Northwest State of United-republic was what I needed when I got kicked out of Arkio for being Lyndon's disabled girl...by a woman called Miriam who said to me: "Repeat prison, please". It wasn't a building I wanted to go in, but Xavier beckoned me into 'Library-Close" from a broken window and my glasses were broken, at the same time! I've got heroine eyes.

Here we go...Anne came. This guy asked me for a lift to buy Perfume then it turns out he has no money so he couldn't so I left him. He's not my responsibility, really? You take the piss out of Death you take the piss out of me. Quite a few too many times it's a way to kill; does it matter...tons and tons:- it's an education to combat death. Yeah, sex is for women who don't add up! Very well, my kind sir let's have dicks on our pain..! But because that is not a chapter in my life; it's a fucking dark absconcion of my will to live. Now how many drugs did you take? Unquestionable amounts of indecision 'Hurry Up' we don't care- do you like my hair... are my ears big? You mustn't disclose your diagnosis or you won't get a job- O blow it in the homestead instead of hurt I got pain! The mad don't get to know their pregnant we tell them when it's done. The brown. When women write, they don't read. Because people don't understand you at all, no. Unless; you have a degree in it.

Are you a doctor? No, are you? No. I'm hired by the police to die.No. I'm hired by doctors. No- I'm a doctor, no I am, no I'm a doctor! I will kill. Jealousy, vaginas, love. No, not to save life but to save. _Drug 'em up to med 'em up to put 'em down_ it's about who puts down the pen first how many pens do you need to feel like a woman?- Pens? No pens, no sex, no. No because my man's safe; he won't section me. I'm afraid it's night now. No, there is no time like the present.

He was a bastard to her. My mother is my friend and I want to leave university behind this is the first chapter of an entirely new book of a book about nature they make you hesitant and then the light goes. And then another out; behind blind sight bird coos. And then another light goes out and a bird flies over her eye. I know why you stared at the sun? Because, *'ici, oui ce qui n'est pas une chose est une chose'*. You don't rape women of their right to sanity and when he entered that room: he was not a good boy he slept well though, owes him. Five hundred dollars a night- the man I never kissed he was a bastard to the most bastard nation. He wasn't nice to her, just when I'm eating it hurts to swallow.. It's hard to live here. Ziclone B: They sent my father to the snow dome for her: love the birds. What's it like; and then- that's the real sign: God, I cannot submit anymore. And when my father walks in access barred. I'm not developing a widow's stoop! You know there are hardly any 'black people' in "Wherever"?! I remember saying that and then my ear came back he's Ella's boyfriend but I listen to the Nth wave. I was trained as my father was- has your money come through yet-Ella loved her father in more ways; I had my period in U.R that's the bulb in the hall that came into my room, the broom stick kiss-

<u>"Having a baby, it's a test in strength."</u>

I am God's swear that God exists. I see highly polished cars. In Hotel *Dieu* there is a God. It's who you hit the ceiling with. Am I a suffering artist committing suicide in the bath? Or are we allowing God's hand in, yesterday- it smelled of orange blossom in here, here I am not writing the blindness papers. Why does my foot hurt or am I just some cheesy footed DOG? When "Love is a hound from Hell"; I saw a blue eyed person on Broadway Street and I leant across to her and she allowed me strangely enough to... Look at a book and see scrawl upon scrawl of someone's writing. Man I'm not a woman. Sorry, about the temporary money and the grapefruit and, man have I seen some Carthages!? Yesterday was sterilily cold I puffed purple smoke out in Northster Park... We remain in the physical! Greylin's Women's Nervos- Centre has a lot to pay for. In this room when I close my eyes I see hurt: I see paving stones:- Icey paving stones.

<u>Dad</u>

Espiritus Sanctus Day: a great bird wung its way past my window yesterday and I ran down the street with water running from my vagina. <u>*Neige Blanche*</u>, in Cole's an Angel resides but they have to stuff the blood back in with, in an angel an Angel resides. According to *Anne the staff* didn't know I was discharged? Why the men, four bastards, in tweed coats on Habitat Road, allow a woman with/ I did the 'I like Prake dance' down Housebound Street, man, it seems like –'*They hunt foxes don't they'*- is happening here; as in 'Four bastard men in tweed coats hunt a beauty like me down'. Get over the toilet sugar! Those are my Father's words... at Strong Street there's a woman who cried and cried and... they take the piss. Women dwell in puffa coats and men are so sterile and dull in this City that they actually walk in to me. A boy, a strange boy, started fiddling, seventeen years old or something:- in front of me as I walked along Armageddon Rd. At precisely 7.25pm: The cold is happening outside, I am 'Pink- Card- Girl' in permanent detention. I see pink coloured paper some places when my eyes are focused on the street- I walk upon the tiles spreading like- brittle fingers clamping round my sinuous neck that ejaculates- a rhythm as I spell my feet alliteratin'-the ground. My bare feet on *THE ROAD*. I can't get myself out. When I die I reside in my body..or do I? Since Lyndon won't socially illicit me. Psychiatry – YOU - are dealing with God's Swear that God exists. Why.

Why are they building bridges in High-Chance, when *I* was there it looked like 'Late'-'Modern'... it was beautiful. Yet in- ' bump into every one Day' : that seem- ed to occur, which it did. **Witch it did** : Fear, anxiety sexual frustration- and that's for men to decipher. Man, do I live in Lightning Bolt but there is a road! But there is a road off of Queen'sway with a roundabout. Just before- the highly polished Roller vehicles roll, named Kindrew's Road. Via the bridge. The bridge at High-Chance Corner. I circle the sick. Do the L shape or do the Ziggy when you walk. Just don't go down, just don't go down. Yesterday what I am ashamed of is in fact, the day 'I spoon-bended it- backwards down'...But then I went down. Last chance-hi-rising!_

At the Ominous... The shower curtain here blows onto me... Jamie Walker...Jay Walker..The Draycott

Mural. One of the most Biblical Bitches in the WORLD is my Birthright to have a life, four: *What goes on...*in mental hospitals is real... For I am a lunatic asylum. Yesterday night, this being Wednesday: there wasn't a single star above the people. The highly polished cars, now I remember Lyra joking, 'Y'- Lyra joked about my glasses, One- Eyed-Motha Fuckin' blind girl- is Zoa. When I'm so poor. Man, stuff of legend. What goes on in mental hospitals is real. It's just the social shitty crap of mouthing up to **Peter the Pepper Pot** who looks like a chocolate muffin. Even the 'word' won't do Justice to this highly processed human being who is writing a book. I hate Thali for naming it in Blank Court, in Blank Court. Listen to Crobert Willyams over the crap phone or listen to me go into a Gek's shop and I remember sleeping under a plastic sheet on Broke~Newington Liye St. And my God, play in the traffic in Dale's Circus there is *Eros*. And yesterday was full of red Double Deckers, or should that be Doppelgangers?

Coz- I am Mass. The sun doesn't shine in Sands much when I am there. My name is No. I am God's swear that God exists. I am God's ball thrower. I do a lot of bone collecting. **Whatev's** -They are my wings. Four IslaTerzoni the world was round her breasts were round for Ella there was nothing, no! 'Four I am Arko'; I said. As I stood on a traffic island. Ruby. Ruby took a photo of me, my name is Cherry Blossom and it falls outside the Council. Englenike is my sanctuary. Every damned indication that I am *'Narcissus and Echo'* so therefore the *vitrines* are the mirrors of my soul and I break spectacles to see them. Sometimes I dream a lonely vision; rainy windows help my arms to see! That which is the soul embrace of a man dressed in a bare skin suit...his body wrapped in my own skin, too. My love, leave the lonely things behind. Remnants of a lonely life... See you there #

Last year the dead fell. I saw Simon on my way to the social ejaculation Unit on Honspey Road. The Police-Station where I used to trot to tell them I lost my Liberty card. 'I lose my Liberty card, Sir. The orchids... Papillion; *Life* is a panoply. I know, I know. Verse 3.31 of the King Jymie Edition of the bible; says- 'Basically this week is totally evil- tripping everywhere yesterday. The grey feathers, St Michael's church- For I am a poor boy- today... you'll find Moses in the poses. I cannot stand social leprosy & the awful walking.

I am in a self containment unit for one person yet. Please don't mess up. So why is my mother's number sometimes socially exclusive and I fear that the socially corrupt want me dead? To touch my book and mum shall wear a red dressing gown. And I went to the launderette where a *"Bitch"* had to touch my clothes inside a washing machine, a social deconstruction aluminium foil washing machine and I heard "Like a pig all stuck with glue". Two folk have been here. All I care about is the safe return of my books from Trey. Because a book is a word. And my mum did her best, all she could do. But I am wearing two contact-lenses in my two eyes. And a man with a pram said "Here I am", and it is in fact all true that the socially distended want me infertile, fat and pregnant in some nascent man's illness called a butch-man's dream or *shumthing* shum-thing. Don't keep doing non-verbals on me for what is a stiff upper lip in this country if it's not a circumcised foreskin?! For God is good, and I shall not see suffering as done with me through my brother. None of its gone which is the beauty of a rock made with stone. "Only because I asked her to." So look after your children, _Philosophie_. What does the Gethitler out of Heaven Girl mean, something inside so strong, S.O.S... So wear a red condom when you fuck me, and "go away unpolites" ? Back to Roger Cruikshanks I shall return 4 living in Lyndon is...Man, I wanted to nick that gay porn.

I am in a self containment unit for one person yet. I always felt guilty after a hangover or, rather, during. I didn't have enough fans-You see! I just felt my back hurt. Desperate to leave the country. For I/ And "I saw Ralph threw his disguise." "They said there'd be snow this Christmas." All lyrics to songs... I have the cassette. Hey, hey nois-ette. 'Tis true. Yes I'm playing it... 18:43pm. "O, the whole world is weird." As said on my tape- "Run, run Reinde- "Yo, Miss Noa" The Little Santa 18:53pm " 'Ere We Go! Anne Came." Yeah: 26/06/20: A scared sari-ed woman came by.

A Compendium of Phrases **"Tear the Voodoo Down/ Blame It on the music/The last time I saw Parys/ Indicted/ Khyto where's the Depth? –Charge/ Yellow roses blooming bare feet who on Earth do y'all think I am?"**

Marylinn. I caught your star. NARK! There are a million eyes but no eyes like there's Ella's! The only face I have is Sylvia's... I hate you so hard sometimes mum said my hair looked –"mad" in Las Pasta café in Cole's & Englenike. Before we made the walk to my home. On a TSO get a JOB Ghetto-**LIFE**. My mother looked elegant today with her dark brown eyes green godly face. I sent my mother off with a big smacker waved to her through the bus windows. Bless the hand that feeds the child. *Benit sois la main qui nourrit l'enfant.* If I can't search for you does it mean you're not their(s). "Oh No-" that's what Simon said. About me & Euan, the builder... As if I'd told about him to Simon in some past made-up. *Amaaazin'* feet Euan has such amazin' feet. That's when I knew I wasn't... Going to have any off-spring.

The faucet is weak keeps me awake interrupts my thoughts, splash-splash/hash. There was a terrible couple walking along Housebound Street, a Fake-Simon and 'me'. And then there was a tremendously fat couple. That walked in front of me. (And they kept walking very slowly ahead of me). I know computer...I love you too.

I am listening to someone else's tape on a BCV hi-fi and it reminds me of good times on the underground with a friend when we debated who was the cooler singer "Disease" or "Sex"? And I put some blue make up on and felt like the tallest woman in the world. W.O.W- we all do our own thing. Don't we. Man, there's a black lamp post up Vinyon's and it's the 2nd of May, just had my injection, love you; you old Arcadian–Maple- Leaf- man. And then again, hope you're OK? It's all about pain up there, towards Northster... I strutted up. Creepy; it was a little. Then I went to the 'Croissant of gold', on Lats Brigade road- really, Severin Sisters. Man, it is so not.

Night: 01.15am *du matin.* I just woke up in *Crevette*-land conduced by the food I had already eaten, a kind of mucky mayonnaise and spaghetti loop *trasvlata,* I was nearly asphyxiated in a nightmare. Gosh, I have never heard of a worse place than Chimn-Minster. Every time I enter a bar and there's men there at the bar; it gets a little cold. Very for me, it was in the Kone's Head tonight. I walked up to Cole's Park and I am depressed because in fact there is a laundry downstairs and whatever is going on with my mother totally incapacitates me... God, the social pressure to write "I hate nervos" is hard.

In Coles, I entered with my lighter, and one of the clandestine said "Here I am". For we remain in the physical. I totally ridiculed them, my eyes wanted to do an eye-roller. My foot hurts. 22:16pm, but at least I have my spaghetti sauce... I hate women. And there really is a launderette downstairs! Despite the fact I wasn't told that at all, by anybody. My mother kept enquiring whether I had been to the launderette.

You breathe, I breathe. My pranayama goes in... In Inglenook it does. And Englenike Council said K'ant – "Can't find my big one's" Go away just isn't enough– *and* I went to the "May-Cure-Cancer-Care Shop"- which is what I call it- and did a Palliative? These are my eyes and this is my body...About 3pm. Silent. And these are my words: And I said to Will "Just Saw God"- Let her sink in, was his response! And then I decided to continue to live in Ingle-nook which seemed ridiculous since, like; Anne, had just *come* in my ROOM- And if you think I'm going *to* have a darned breakdown then drive a car- And I: Englenike Van 3pm! Bad driving ? And when I close my eyes I do not see what you do- I do not see what you do. 999 Englenike car 3pm... I AM AN ANGEL BUT I RESIDE IN THE PHYSICAL WORLD! I envisage Anne as an alien in a pink ruff, no! As I hope... that gravels really hard for my.

Went down the wastes and brought a computer from Djemil on a Monday: fear itself !

"I'm going to New Rork. They pray slaves..."

Something mysterious about the Square, always receiv-
ing messages:- little synchronicities. Actually Euan's *so*
cool, socks with sandals yeah, m-8! Except he doesn't
fit in with my way of seeing. Sometimes I'm O.K. I wish
I could be less paranoid-double, split, polarized / "in
my thoughts". And the bathroom is empty there's just
make-up. And Euan's 'evil' residue. Cute guy but the
language barrier's just getting too much. There's no
carpet here and the thing with Rav last night was weird.
Fancying him and yet; of course- Euan! Dark scorched
eyes- wild brown-hair- swollen; red lips. Cute men...
went in Rav's room with the dream catcher on the wall
which is a mix of shells and a mini red letter box on
strings. Also, an old lamp from some antique shop,
films everywhere. I hung out in there. It's quite a
phenomenon to *fuck Ella*. "You must get some sweet
relief feelings that that's not you- it's me!" Went in
Rav's room some brown haired beauty was breathing
in/out, under a duvet. Did it feel cool to have them
round? Actually it was good. Inda too.

Me and Robert

You don't know what you know pimp. For Thali
wherever I may find her...Letters from a Chicken Firm.
Tom D; my friend; is the justification that mental health
"Problems" don't exist. He thinks now that he knew
"Kim-Kool" when he was a kid. He might have done.
In actual fact his guitar's named after her. I don't know
if he'd *mind* me disclosing his guitar's name-sake:

'Kola'..? Oh sorry did I get that wrong?! He looks cool, *maaan*. He's got a good radio said his name "Tom Desmonds". Haha! Tricky's also his favourite word.

And I'm scared and feel somewhat vulnerable- since I have witnessed other people's Abusive Verbal's quite a bit. And people are mucking about, around my coat and I hate the T.S.O. And I miss Simon, and then again. It seems like the entire world seems to be involved in my book.

24th of April

We emit time when we breathe. I'm smoking a cigarette. And I'm TSO'd... "It doesn't give you confirmation that it saves... on this computer." Man, the dead fell. I know th---Tyronne has my book. I can't write "They". And I know so.

19th November

I reacted badly to the *Contingency plan*. I'm worried because I cannot find my computer charger. Might go to get suitcase back from Rav and Euan... Can't find extra part of SIM for my phone. So it looks like birthday wishes may well... simply happen online.

Anne Came.

"And there are four realities..." Seductive, no.
Irritating, yes, Maman.

Sunday the 14th of May: I'm stopping smoking/ Don't feel so healthy. Met Marco and Josepo last night at

Dolphin sq. Lost my phone and unable to contact anyone for a day! Had my last cigarette for the day..! How I'd ideally like to wake up:- herbal tea, coffee, toast, oil burner, play a yoga DVD. Or go to yoga classes. And volunteer with Cris in Haight St Park. Book a ticket to go to U.R. Villette to go and see Fred-o.

I asked her to do it, or what the Hell Lyndon- why is there a 73 bus going down cripplin'g Saint street, since when? So much I love him, "so much I love him" yeah actually I cannot stop thinking about the Lock. Justin's lock which is his hideous mouth, the scream, the footballers outside! The prop of Simon outside his house, a man...That looked the spit of him and when was that? The day I named the people, the day that was beautiful. I'm so lonely. And the Lascole police. I'm intelligent.

"Sum superhero, sum super human gifts and that's at Hero's desist." Played the radio 20.39pm; I'm in the dog pound, Honspey Road Reception Centre." Put down for what? I'm really getting off on the title "Je Suis Un Ange" because in fact it's called *"Romeo et Juliette"* Part 1, sequel.

Feel pressure because-"Really, Riley"- I'm a painter. *Je suis un peintre, mais vraiment je suis ..* But angels don't fly, that's a lie; they appear in people's dreams. They appear in people as hallucinations, but *vraiment c'est une-* Catastrophe, I'm an angel, they are idiots 'cause really humanity you are from the sea! *Manatees.*

Water's Daughter:

Five bats are around my head. The man has a pigeon in his eye. And you with the "Golden Scissors"- that you wield! I need a dictionary, not the Bible where *Quando*

Celi put the Ottoman Empire to rest. White dove: because what's O.G.D but G-H-D, but God. Deus, *la Bis.* And *"Les pim-pons"* goes on in the background. *J'ai faits signe,* what's a signet ring doing in my candle wax: "Oooooouuuuui Elllaaaaaaaa". Xmouth Sweet. On Strong Street there's a room... Your days are numbered.

Written on a paper bag in Lapo Ward; Northster: February.

I walked the streets of Lyndon... unlocking it so to speak! Did a giant 'I like Prake' dance down Housebound Street, Broke~belle library was mental, the night before I sheltered...as I was homeless. They sang: "We are health-foods and we shall love!" Only slices of clementine. Then Quazi Road turned into a shit-shop soul, shake down party. Then I urinated in front of a Unionist Chapel. I should be slightly ashamed. I'm in Lapo ward bricking it a bit; Tracey, Nona and Mum shall come and visit you.

Pushed, loved, at The Protagonist's Crossroads. We understand. It's my hiawasca moment. I had to say I was a paranoid schizophrenic to stay in a flat which is temporary accommodation; of course. In fact it was framed as a "crap studio". Don't play the one legged violin do ya? I've written a book, Paul and -Pete Fast- did the diddle on me he already had the deposit -for someone else.

Which is why Munroe Rules:

I'm writing *"Marilynn's"* book. Question: What is electricity harnessed from? Answer: a harness.

You stand to stare at a "cherry muffin" Girl: tell her the time of day, and I see you and when-I see you "I love you." Think you can daub? In a way, that's painting with your shit. I'm thinking about hurt and in a way that's what dogs do. They take it up the arse from their mother's; says, like: the last cigarette I smoked. Sitting in a blue-painted room. I came here not to feel pain when this merits "old". So it takes awhile to know: assimilate where I am; after you've been sectioned as many times as me! What you come? I will hurt you until I see the light because I have seen the dying, yeah, the man with the glassy eyes said that. He also claimed I stole their pastille. People don't change expression; you know when they laugh out-loud in a Franzien's-Era tower block. When tears come they flow... Do you know why I don't sleep with a pillow because I am *sickness* itself. They put plasters on tears. Plaster casts for fears...So, I don't go out much..But man, when you say that in the saddest voice in the world... I feel so exasperated with you: I look about me at that moment: Books should make you happy when you read them not like slavishly gulag all over them. Which is why Munroe rules. Love poem written on a strait jacket: *"Threw the disguise. I love flowers. Ever seen two swans flying. Which is why."*

What, I suddenly thought of my brother...

Strong Street- And they get a vacuum out they don't-they do it on purpose. Sunday you don't take the piss through my mother-Halalu! They knock their own door.. 1.20am and they try and defend themselves. *You* don't use as they put the bag in the hall and you try and you blame us for what you do. Ten to One. They are total freaks you think *Fuck* is the name for God. 1.25am They slam the door and then vacuum inside their house and they make 'loud siren noise' and stop. And probably two people want to come in. "I would have liked to known you." Elbo Joan. Salty wind. You do not go gently against the dying of the light. Pluck-the- moon- from- your- heart get a test tube out and call it Ella. *Nutzjobbies.* And what time did the ambulance find him. Do you grow a dick in Massifburger? Nicki grew stick! I love you. Sound of the alarm, purple-light-disco- crosses that have no name. The "Ten R- us" Project. Gita's dying. I am A.A. I did know a thing or two about women who hate men when they come down alone and invest the whore population with their infection which is drugs. And that's for eventual discharge. Council flat in Lyndon and money to get out because what are houses for but to come out of?

Doing Crack was the best thing I ever did according to my mother which is why I won't be one. Because of men who get girls they...want, just because they say I don't want to **bam**. I love you for always. I saw a fox today- ever come to Thali's house stayin' for three days. Until I go blind to my own beauty. Nightmares-Inner: Wax came for a reason. There's no reason for madness and there's no reason for combating it with psychiatry which is why I need help for some reason...no. But then again, no is never enough. It's their job to get you sectioned on an almost permanent basis. Which is not why phone's are important which is why nothing's temporary. To look for love is utterly futile when you're sectioned for 4 months because you don't listen because you're not bored or boring. Because I'm interesting. *Because.* Oh yeah. Because it is a good idea! Oh what's the idea-oh… Yes. Oh. Really? I mean I'm writing on envelopes but the wrong way round. Can you smell it too? Because it implies you are ugly very, very. That's the only sense that seperates us. Do psychiatrists doodle? No they draw. Call it art. Call it charts.. Pictures of people's heads and say they're unwell. To investigate a pleasant person is to ruin their life. That's not thinking that's drawing Ella…

What is art- but yeah. Isn't it? I wonder if you can give us a clue. Tricky. Yeah. Why bother. Why bother? Which is why psychiatry nicked your art. Oh, it's about art, no it's about history, no it's mine. *Isn't* enough. To investigate a crime…It's about sharing the table- at dinner; at breakfast. We set the rules buy their standards. If you don't have patience to read then why write because I can't. You tell me not to smoke which is why I do. Pictures move when I look at them because I'm an artist, the men won't let me go and get my flower stalk out of the bin which is why I'm single! Do you know what a *"Nice"* biscuit is? It's a nice biscuit served by a cookie served by a chocolate *"Bourbonne"* served by a monkey:-It's a bit weird; it's still poetry. I'm not implying anything, by sitting here in silence well, it would be nice to be heard. Well it would! I don't hear I don't speak; in order to invent my own.

We don't stare at the sun in here. We don't stare at the son- we do. Women scare children / men don't; men do scare. You don't know what you don't. If anything I'm against the law- I'm just in. Now no, you're not.

The lights are on the sun's out. Come out the light... is on, is. It; you don't...

"Do you know why Sheikhs of the Sub-sub continent were fearful of "the smell of "Grey Feathers Smell" because those people were the first to see the stars. Women can be: "non-verbal men", verbal, orators. Women are givers. God's a telescope." Excerpt from my diary 12/15

5.30:

You listen in on my words because I am silent...Trooped me.. Bottles move outside because I said a compliment to...Spastic hairbrush so now we know she's... No, it's not part of the family because of temporariness and then. I live in myself because I smoke cigarettes; ash drops onto crockery; they do it- and then we think about the objects in our mother's room. 5.50 By breathing too heavily she knows she's dead. 5.45 You push that curvy girl too far with music! "Four" a nothing and all "Eye" wanted was a threesome! And so you bleed the sick. But really I'm writing *"Love's-Lost-Highway"*. Relations, denominations, a curve of purpose and my baby's core. Glue...Spit. So take the fat. Slam that. Spoon feed me an apple a day. Geezer. Spit, glue, true. Hospital-High, Lyndon. 5.36pm

Yeah it went well. Leave perhaps... Chlor- mental note and a pine injection, one once a month isn't it? The lips that read, the pages that see. No man is an island. No man is in Ice/Land. God, there are three that inspire inside the tavern! Peter, Paul and John. Ponce Pilate's day is it. Getting all biblical? 8.00 It's near impossible for any woman to write a book and then you say I'm a racist and then they move the Word, tears drip into my mouth;- remembering and then it turns back into... do you have a girlfriend..how to turn a *homo* into a lesbian.

The poor to see through men abused. I was blind so I can: See I can;- see you through the blind! The blind can't see: *the blind can see* it is their choice not to *see*. Do you know what Psychiatry is? The blindness game. The blindness game we can see you're not well...Why: how, how can we see when we can't see when it's cold dark gloomy through our imaginations. I can see you. *O an imaginary love*. I eat dead people. You're off your head, Ella. No, I'm a dog to the police. I am! And yeah you want to go to hospital mate! I mean why is there an age of consent for death when I fucked myself up quite a few times?!

Person A: Actually she's the abusive one. Doctor B: No, she is. Person A: No, you are. Doctor B: Yeah! A and B: Who picks up the gun first?...

Please read the pain-Reduction-Handbook. Basically I've been through so much violence in my life, I don't want to die but man, when I go into psychiatry... I'll be dead, actually! Are the neighbours giving oral-sex to people? With a hoover...er, highly commendable! No I... Through the noise maybe? You're not going to play a nightmare on her. Nor on me; nor on I, nor on anyone you fucking sacrosanct- *Bitch!* Love and you be the judge. Do you like women? Not at the moment... maybe, never maybe- I will? Maybe I won't. Some people do... maybe I'll die. It is actually like dying but. "*Wot's*" psychiatry for, no, it's for the poor to see through men abused. Oh?

What happened to me at 39c, Strong Street, Englenike, Lyndon

John: taking the skin off her *'brudders'*. What does that mean…I find it hurts to swallow and there was Paul and there was Frank and you think that's a good time? 5.30pm For I gave Olligan blue phone and that's the real I. You don't take the piss of the skin I'm in. Because love comes too. And then a car speeds past outside; and he's filling the air with smoke and he closes the front door first, and then he stands outside and. Snoring, voices… and then you hear footsteps. *"They're listening in on an angel."* 6.05: Knock on the glass. Listening to *me through my eyes!* The noises in here are so loud and you don't cut mine off. Listening to the social derivative- so I grope and scope around but for Moha I was rich- Play with Misty the cat under the covers- I decide who'll heal, she'll give you up…And then they shut the door and blow air into… and then someone hawks up outside . Whip it skitzkitten! Let's take the cat away from…*Banglash* her. I see the light that shines inside men… You don't take three pages off someone's face. And they stop to listen to someone eat! And now they know I'm listening to the time 6.10 as it ticks. You exist to make a trap for Ella about Olligan; her dad. Oh: but because we listen to your thoughts we know. So then three men walk out leave the door open so that person becomes more beautiful than you.

And that was what it was like to live at Strong Street and bathe the room in my tears and write on envelopes instead of having children to "throw their shit stained nappies into an already overflowing bin…" and make noises that drove me wild with distress- in a narrow hallway next to weird people in winter time in Lyndon. I climbed in through my window as the lock got broken by them on my door. The walls were very thin so noises and electricity mattered... It was a cold, dark place that still remains somewhere, nestled on a leafy street in Englenike. One beautiful thing about that street were the birds that flew down it and hopped about. At least I had a net curtain but the neighbours would congregate outside and tap, tap my window...

30th December: And then a car drove past and they keep religion to themselves. You don't turn police into please. When you see me you look at me through broken glasses and then he rectifies the ejaculat that I need to deep throat! Your days are numbered. And then you shove the word in their mouth and you look at all the taboo around you. And he's a bad, sad man and I say: "Keep 'em chained through the ink tank"- and then they shove the word in that. Raise 'em high to put 'em down to kill the child of God; it's invented by animals to keep the smog clean that never saw the light of day! Stop feeding me lies. You don't touch my black coat and bag and smugly smile because I don't smoke. No you don't. Olligan my blue phone. *I writ' what are seeds for Pip,* all the queuing up are standing. We are still in the putative stages of : "Get the fuck out of "Yessir Animal-fat's house." You don't tap on the glass. Swallow the ice-cream that mothers never die. When you see me you look at me through broken glasses. You don't look at *"Arthur's* naked body in a onesie."

That's what disabled meant: No dick girl. What is sex if it's not a mental health problem for me. That's why I think of my childhood when I have sex with

Moha because mum doesn't approve. The mad make the best mothers on Earth. Born! We believe they are born, no, *they're made that way*. It's decide we shall. Take that chicken shit out of your eyes. Doesn't matter... And that's a shadow passing through. Does psychiatry commiserate. No, it contemplates your thought for you. But then if someone really takes to you...Can you, do you hear their voice? Or do you just hear their voice or do you contemplate or think before you speak or do you just. Does a psychiatrist say -"Don't worry, I'm on a tranq, too". No, never. All psychiatrists say. Let's prescribe her. Get our thinking helmet on and call her mad; a doctor said that. It's a second... Generation drug. Woo! Because no one believes you because: "I'm God." Signed with love; psychiatry. *39c Strong Street CONTINUED:* They made me say the word window in here and then they said the *vitrines* are coming back to you. You do cut my jealousy off a good looking girl like you should wear glasses to write a book. 10.20pm 30th Dec: He hurts the body inside of me and then I... and then he says he's important and then he says hair's not the same as skin. And that's a lie he's socially regressing me... so you give her a cigarette to turn the brain into a body. *Mike* said Abe-Coal-Mine some sort of secret code... and; nodded. He's doing the white –dollop-chocolate.

Gone to the bank, no appointment actually today lots of pressure to work, somehow to make some art. Losing my ex was a blessing in disguise yes it is true, the more I don't want him the *best* I feel. We stifled each other... the sex life was uptight and hurt... I no longer want to see him too. I think I can buy a typewriter and write in Dolphin square and by the national or the

Ingle's museum or Artgallery#2 or "Late NITE'S" or Velium's Cinema, the White-ish Sq whatnot. Be good to get out and about, portraits too. Drawings. I remember Mr. Vince's suggestion of filling a suitcase full of my art; or my old outdoor easel to paint outdoors. And outside café TAO too. I'll need business cards made...

I swim in my head

Pink sunset in the sky; across Severin Sisters and Honspey Road, the crisp delicate score of a plane's white marks. White clouds left bereft in the atmosphere of glowing pink and highlights of orange...Up in the skies. A cobalt blue sky, today the sun's hot and as the tortures go; I checked to see if my ex had left me completely yet...I understand myself as a ...Matthew's blank. The Fish cake. Else. Bell. Point. Star. Quizo. Bus stop candle wax Tom- stick –sawyer: I Bet Fred. Else. New O Slaves. Get _Zoe_ Out Of Heaven Girl. Go through Hell to get her not to drown "Ohio" Man. Hey Columbus, whose Frankie. Saint of Acids. I'm a writer really, Wryly, Serious? _Sirius_ is a star, Ella. Armageddon: slave- ships tombs- spout-_he will never get out_. Literacy; the wor(L)d. Jude was slave driver's daughter. She's mining Cain, Cain's pine. Don't take the meds-Ella! Grandpa; I am star/ smoke/ wine/ thunder/ powder: Broken window and my glasses were broken! I've got a heroine's eyes.

Poem:

Last night was so cold / I murdered someone/ to get AIDS in me to sort the/ thrombo out- Beggar man boy...5p coin/ War outside/ Joonsbury's Central. Jo slapped her / about. Hugged dead A.A man / Thali turn it into ice. High Bangs Lower pharmacy/ yesterday.

And then he said; "AND THAT'S YOURS BABE- > - THAT'S YOURS BABE- THAT'S YOURS- THAT'S ALL YOU GOT:- THE FACE OF AN ENORMOUS PAST in CAR- INSURANCE- MAN'S LAPIS-BLUE EYES."

<u>Coralei.</u>

The curtain is swinging, in Ingle-nook they play the ice-cream van a lot. Wait for Joey to text. Where, when, what and if. Robert's lost his 'phone. What's she doin' the washin' up for? No-one's coming in! Why bother... *well I am*. Oh, Euan Smith what a *pretty pretty boi...* One of the angels no-less than you or I. Pink top and white shorts. Tom, Smith and me; Ella; are going to the Ponds. Enter the sub-aquatic. Eagle'd eye-moon. Grey shoes by the dance floor. Oh! Dolphin Square I love you. Dark hairs growing back on blonde; I need you baby! Shake, rattle, roll 'em. *"Y'all -are –a- lot -a trampz –on- ma'-beauty!"* Thinking of the homeless man or rough-sleeper under the train line outside Blow-away Rd station. Of all the stations there are; is he waiting to die? He sleeps and never gets up. Once I saw him begging, kind of waving his hands. His language is mine... Good-looking, despite the dirt on his clothes and face. And Will. The young man who I said "Just Saw God" to. Will lying on the pavement outside supermarkets. Just stopped.

Just Saw God. I know the lyrics. *Bless* the arms that carry the child in... Went down "City/Slide" the way *Euan* calls it; and met a girl called "Ringo" once....All those walks to Olifant park paid off, actually it was about twice I went. Damn you fear… Fat bitches screw up my place! *Hanna* and Moustafa Gabor or whatever her name was…Yeah. All those walks did pay off; went down along Urchin Street and looked at the mural by her; "Quince up my Tart";- no less. Saw the painted mask of Death she'd painted there and at first I scanned over to the left almost immediately across the other people's painted faces and saw a woman; wearing, like; a band around her head and on it was daubed *"NO MORE WAR"*. Now, I don't know if I'm pronouncing it right! It felt very significant on the walk home like a blessing. If the bastards come round once more and section me I'll stab them. *Ill bitches.*

Actually thinking about Simon is a complete waste. The big mirrors of the swimming pool loomed large and my reflection in them seemed to flood them. I skulked past, avoiding a glance; as I neared his house. The orange street-lighting fluttered in corners whilst the trees pulsed, aching in the dark. I placed a photo of myself in a small bundle tied up with yellow ribbon through his post-box. "Life has so much more to offer." My mother's words or, are they mine? Such as the decision not to ring my mum I think I talk to her; maybe…too much? *"Just go with your heart."* She seems to incant.

I think to myself I have fifty quid and need to buy a camera. Send my nieces a present too, soft plastic ducks and the 'Lost/Leaves' DVD, a tacky card and a Lyndon gift bag. I vaguely recall pretending that Simon and I were high- after and during sex with him. That we were both high on heroin… I took the story as far as inventing a tourniquet! In the distance a child is screaming its voice melds with the CD I'm playing.

"I swim in my head. *Vade's War / God's a black man:* I'm an angel. An anonymous who saved me taught me you breathe... I breathe / Thanks for the "Turner"-Esque sky Dad; and "Marilyn" did my mirrors./ Nothing can make me suffer./ Nothing is set in stone (everything changes). I'm going to change my name, / I'm adopted sadly, and I am the swear that God exists. / "...*Signed:* Ella"

You don't read into a book to read the future: Let's bring a car here and slam the doors all the time on Strong Street and then another punch and then slam the car door and drive off. Ingle-nook stole Ella's book from her green bag in a pub, once... Monday T.V 10.12am 30.01.47: *Sickly* muslins and a tobacco scarf at High Bounds Road.

This was the start of a potential new relationship based on friendship. "A girl with a towel turbaned around her wet, "freshly showered" hair stands above me by a hair's breadth. She smokes a cigarette, cup of tea in her hand, she wears; what looks like a *mini* dressing gown...it being... half open. *Supposedly* slumming it I sit as she stands and smokes. I get up to leave and as I enter the building, "...I think"

All my family aren't calling me. Robert: no. Mum: no. It's like weird..? (as if... I'm not allowed a boyfriend; based on the past).. Joe was heavy on the good things to do with my being strong! And then I thought "Danger, in relation to the girl; and that was why I didn't talk. Saw some flashing lights on the road and thought they were the police." *Shifty*. As Tyronne /Joe said, also "You're stronger than you think". It's as though the family members can't condone me having a *"boyfriend/relationship?"*

Whether to meet Joe later or not. Yesterday I would have said yeah definitely, it's all in my head, why not? I want to, it's just I've got to do the washing up, get the papers ready, go to the bank tomorrow, top-up my phone, meet at 3pm. Clean the room. I've got no money think I'm getting too much of a good thing. Well, he's not all that clean. Why can't he be perfect? Be good to see him anyway. Feel like people think he's a loser. He's cool. Saw *Mary* from the 'Lascole Police' incarcerating somebody else this morning. I have to be careful... Maybe I'll say I'm on my period as to avoid having sex in the hostel. What about *Tyronne*, or rather Joe and him having a problem with me seeing other men! Tyronne's cool about... it but Joe isn't. Well, the overall thing is to protect my "mental".

"NORTHSTER or/ ALL MENTAL HOSPITALS.

I never want to go there again. It would render me totally incapacitated. The red, the yellow and the blue. I would've written 'or'. But when there's no choice drugs are an option only! So I spent the whole day chuckling to myself, went to Cole-Look Bridge Park and saw two magpies. Bumped into 'O' who was smoking drugs the other night when I was there with 'F'.

Life's tragic. Man yesterday was so weird... Think I'm in love, had my photo taken by a real-live photographer then I went mad and raced through the streets of the state of Peach, or should that be; from the world-Renowned State that is the City o' Lyndon's, well, we'll leave that blank. What followed was; I ripped a poster down. Kaye and I have things in common- we're both mad. He calls me "*Cherry*'" there is some comfort in being surrounded by people that let off their mortal remonstration too. "Maz" I caught your star, got told the fattest compliment that I look like "Marillyn" from Oona the tramp-lady of St Peter's Church. Joe looked spiffing, in Dolphin Sq. Got to recuperate my book from my mother. Got to make *some- art.* Now I've run out of money I don't know... Buy cheap art materials?

- I wrote part of the book over time from April 21st Twenty-20 after having been discharged from hospital. It's all stuck together! And they are pieces; *of experiences recalled from memory,* and also written immediately afterwards; and, or a while later on recollection. The contents incorporate writing written at 39 C Strong St in Darnden. That was the street that the green and also blue; birds flew down. Keeping the time as I wrote; time was important to my writing as situations happen-*stanced* while I wrote.-

Interview located at The *Rouble's* Pub: "May; next year" by "MELANIE DAVIS"- Hope I don't... ARE YOU AN ARTIST? NO I'M A MIRROR TIME. WHAT SKIN COLOUR ARE YOU- NO I'M A GREY. WHAT SKIN COLOUR ARE BLACK MEN- THEIR SKIN IS RED You don't decide that with drugs do you: yes actually you do. Which ones do you take? I smoke joints and occasionally cigarettes. Sex is for squares which is why drugs are good. Do you know what space is, it's a hesitation.

30th December !

Witch means The Tiny Flynn's Resto' Christmas. PSYCHIATRY IS CRITICAL and what's to criticize, all men practicing are tramps. Which is why I don't need to love because I'm a psychiatrist. Ella's SONG IS the saddest song in the world. Why, because it is true she is YOU. YOU *ARE* not going to like this but they stole my wallet. The PERSONAL "INTERNATIONAL" ALLOWANCE WHICH MEANS I AM DISABLED; when a blood infection is considered a disability in this country because a blood infection makes you handicapped-because your mum moved to Sifar at an early age and you can't- oh yeah? Pluck the moon from your heart and get a test tube out and smash it and call it Ella because *IRATE* is a shit world called "Special" which means, I am. Where are you, special…Where are your specializations? I work. On Strong Street there is a woman. Oh really? Ella your letters aren't touching Darla's the pregnant woman's at Strong St? Are those letters touching? Darla's? Are those letters touching Darla's- "No." IF YOU COME TO MY PARTY DRESS-ED IN A PANDA SUIT YOU'RE NOT ALLOWED TO COME TO MY PARTY. No, it's because I actually grew up and realized that inanities are psychiatry's *PRID QUO-QUO*. Do you know what a panderer is a disgusting word which has many…IN SANITY I WON'T DIE BUT IN GRIEF I WILL…IN HOSPITAL I WILL DIE. SUICIDAL IDEATION ABOUT THOUGHT. W.T.F: ARE YOU ON? A THOUGHT! Key words: "Charlemagne, football, psychosis and glue" Which is what Lyndon's made of. "HATE"- why do they make you think of your brother?

It's other men who do. It's mothers who won't have '*em*. Which is why you can't have it. Don't quince up my tart. Yeah do you know what a mince pie is? I couldn't give a shit. Welcome to the STIFLERS; where you can't smoke... to somehow learn to somehow get the fuck out. In order to get out of an institution you have to learn the rules there are no rules where you get hit! (Hits)! Where you can die- They're all answers to telephone calls. MADNESS DOES NOT EXIST ONLY EGO DOES. Only out of fear do...everything. Or? Lapkin man is it? A cigarette. MANNERS MAKETH MAN. Women don't have manners 'THEY' have MANORS. Do you spit or swallow, no I wallow in tears when I go in there...IT IS RAPE yeah they're from my head and they're accurate too- you're in psychosis Ella you're making art. DUE TO HISTORIES YOU CAN'T SMOKE INSIDE A HOSPITAL BUT YOU CERTAINLY CAN IN A MENTAL HOSPITAL WHERE IT'S NOT CARE IT'S HELP- IT'S NOT CARE. IT'S "*AU SECOURS*'" "OH SECURITY!" FOR SALE IS HARD...FOR A WOMAN WHO CAN SELL HER BODY. BUT WHAT ARE DRUGS FOR? TO SELL BODIES AND TO SELL DRUGS. TO BODIES? THAT DON'T WANT THEM. I ACTUALLY LOVE LYNDON, BUT I'M NOT ALLOWED TO LOVE LYNDON BECAUSE WHEN I AM IN LYNDON...You're figuring stuff out.

Love Letters from a Chicken Restaurant:

The world renowned chicken chain... My special episode or spiritual episode or spiritual experience? Moha is a bad guy. Tyronne's a cool man because he says "I love you" to me. Missed old friends and went to West Street or somewhere the gaff where Tyronne lives. We live in our world(s). Don't we *just*. My authorship fantasy is to land myself a place. Somewhere to go. Cool CD gotten from a friend, boredom and dwindling dreams. Dreams of getting away. Sexy fuck is 'e ? Chuck A might have said-"*You don't know what you know, Ella*". Sun's shining, rain water drops, rain pierces the awning, we shelter *grimacing* all the way. "Ella; a lot happens." I can only imagine. What's it like to be "a-not-her" person! Then you see the light that shines, besides that's the only way. Only the lonely and destitute go to food banks. Wear a skin! See how the bare shines... writing trying to claim some authorship back, some credit from some barely light-able candle wick. I'm waiting and I'm seeing things, things that *aren't there*. What does that mean, some such "mad shit" ? Dolphin Sq, saw Joe. Good guy and that's just a bad lip. May meet him tomorrow to sleep with him, three o'clock sharp.

<u>Immanuel Kant, Saint Augustine. Slippery kiss.</u>

"I swim in my head." It was said by me, on Housebound St some days ago, the computer just interrupted. Basically the computer just interrupted me! I went out for a walk, and spoke to some bastard...And the Bridge in Northster isn't being built. Basically, ten to eight... Oops, *Dad* is GOD. I saw a dog talk, and rap music is brilliant, in fact all music is brilliant. Do I live with *"Franklin. D.Hoover"* or are all of you lot out to kill? A single angel. I saw millions of people judge me today or something...and you don't cut off a bloodline. In fact the dog did an angle at me. As I walked up to death itself...i.e: the Hospital. And I see *little twigs on the pavement and the folk want proof I'm-* I've got forty three minutes to save this in- "Yesterday /All my Dreams seemed so.../ Far Away." Nigel; "little eggs" leads to; broken glass. Walk anywhere. Jazz bunny ears, my favourite flavour of pink. No way cheese foot! Me in this plagiarist City. Lyndon owes me. Lyndon owes me: Chocolate, cheese and sandwiches for. Sometimes it stinks. I stuttered- What you're not allowed to do; those are my eyes, this is my body. Brutal/Trap-Door... In the City you're not allowed to "flick" the bird: I discover this on a perpetual basis. I saw Tom Jeynes on Altheight Barn. I saw my old school teacher who looked asleep when I met him, I saw my mother rub her tired eyes-"I've lost my "Marylin's"." I said out loud which meant my breasts at the time:- Her name is Ella and only...Only the cool. I named the city, I named the squalor. This is a woman in chains. Can't you see!?

Penile cars, my red lipstick in Lorenzo's dark and brittle hands. Youseff died or did he just have cheese-foot? No, he died. In Hell pack horse blower 20001 after the death of the little boy on Strong Street. In Ingle-nook there are flowers, tulips and to lose is... At the Archille Express-o; there's a man buys a wonderful cubed chicken wrap and "Four we endorse Khyto where's the Dhepth?" When "We" touch food we say that openly in front of my body. On Saturday May 6th we are injecting Ella with a secret substance that being poison, in Ingle-nook this is done. By sin, in Ingle-nook we openly stink. What's that smell?

Art-Project:

I'm a harpoonist. As a child I was a teenager, as a woman I was *Mein*, I was mine. In my womanhood I found Christianity. I seem to be permanently stuck with the residue of the Munlley Craw asylum. "One eyed blind girl. Means your beautiful." Angel in disguise. So, yeah this is hard to write, because other people including you dear computer are *fuggin'* it up for me.

PEOPLE IN LYNDON ?

I'm going to a land so far away. They pray. Slaves they are, they that are right. Have a boy…Get pregnant. So, I met Gael at the doctor's. On a "Lyndon-Ting day." Pleasant enough- a severely *autistic* guy or at least with a bone wasting disease he was. He was in his wheelie chair I leant over to look in the mirror that he had had placed for rear view, or something. He also had a mirror sort'a sticking out in front, an appropriate comm-unication tool for someone so thin as he, and he looked at me. His face was shocked, his mouth open, he had a look of confusion in his eyes. I smiled, hoping he wouldn't; back at me. I reached my hand to cover my left eye to do a *Non Verbal* at him but in a way a deeply Christian thing overtook me instead I done and gone said: "Don't take the eye-broken out of me" and as I covered my eye to add a body language to the perplexing transference this sentence would impact to 'Gael' I looked up above me; into all the *G.P's Surgeries's in the World's* windows and saw my only self reflected back at me in more than a dozen mirrors reflected on and on until all "Eternity" seemed to elapse around me and I felt a great rose open within me and blooming; as if it could! Me. A woman smiling blind. Hesitantly I stiffened myself and with my hand still covering my left eye I leant forward. I saw he was sun tanned and tall though ensconced in a true chariot! "Done up in brocades." Sort of lanky; like a basketball player probably is? I have no way of telling but something inside me hoped for the best for him, truly. On entering, later he used the lift. I hoped he wouldn't get stuck.

I met Martin outside the Clamdigger's. Nice guy and that, just too fast a talker for me. When all I want to do is 'S'-cream. First thing I noticed go, was my breathing, as the pine socially remonstrated me for smoking cigarettes. I walked down onwards past Optician's where I had brought the eye-drops. And outside Tunshi's Maquette it was dark, dark as the day it could have been. I walked down Lytherbird Rd passed the socially leprous. "How many of *y'er* family are you carrying? Quite a few, about five," I thought internally. They fly above my head, four bats and one is my muse. There are five women in the hospital named "Axe-Downdoom". And as I enter this temporary accommodation I cannot relax, I feel the muzzle of a dog and smell its stench, or rather, darling; its wet coat. When once I smelt orange blossom. I hear the typing in front of me, of someone else typing, it does not stop even as I stop; even if there's no-one there. It stops and stutters and tries to distract. I walk through a Ghetto it starts at the gas station, on the cobbles. But I'm getting out- a council flat. *Really?* Yes- make that her palliative the thought before the thought that I should write *palliative*.

The Year: So time just stopped. Hours and hours of endless conversation with a public health (Low Rd) named Annie who stole purple ducks from Strong St "The Massacre", the rape; the lobotomy! Where Mike had sex with "No Dick" disabled girl El. Have all the men in my life been *utter tossers*?! So I'm still T.S.O'd and they've got signs with *"violent "* or *"aggressive behaviour"* on their doors and they sectioned and criminalized me, put me away and were to throw away the key. But I still found a way...through decorating my flat and making art...and yet, *what for* ?

10.02pm Kicking back, the light's on: the bulb and in the background the radio's on in "ROOM 28" Honspey Road, Lyndon and it smells of cooking. Raga raps from some continent are singing: *"O, let's not be alone. Let's be shell fish, baby...Tonight; I just hit the Liquor Store in Stratten-Lang"*, and then she describes. *"Lesbe shell..."* "Grewwsum Toothsome" is a boring ass wipe by the way. And so it's adverts for Telecom's 2 Infinity season in the shark-Tank. I come to the conclusion that: "Heaven's personal." And in my head I think this, alone.

Prayer:

Long black gloves and a crack addict or a dealer and a crack addict.

Question) Are You gay? Question) Have you read the Bible? Before entering the eponymous "Lunatic Asylum", these are two questions one should ask.

Englenike, Lyndon, Ingle-nook *"Nicht Rauchen"* The day I escaped: The paper cup. The day of denial times x100. Fireworks didn't go up in the sky- could until then? *Mary Baird*. At twenty nine why couldn't I stay? And then Justin came into the picture. *"Wahgwhan"* was said as the man greeted me. He was a white male stereotype at the rotating doors of "Peach's" swimming pools, *"good lookin'"*. Yeah, so I went out without my cigarettes, and then I was at the launderette... and "They" touch cloth before they yield...I found that extremely disgusting, once I was outside a lost place.

WTF, I was a bit off score! You soften my body then you put your hand in then you re-engorge and then you come back to me, *O my Ell's. I've always known there was something about the sun and me and you; so, like when I realised that was in fact in Lyndon.* My shadow is my own... O sweet cherry blossom falls. Basically, I'm wearing two contact lenses and I have two sockets yet one eye, which is weird. Tim, you looked amazing today, all tough and frisked.

Men R Women 2: Arch High Mickey looked like shit. In fact he did and all. What was that guy looking like an actual fish from the so-called; "I swim in my head day"...? Outside Fountayne Place or the 'Chowdhury Centre' I stopped to think; I've got to stop worrying about getting in touch with old "friends" because they're not worth it. "Oh shit, I died." should be written in neon pink glowing tube or whatever- *so to speak in Dutch I am not a receptacle for abuse from strangers...Nik Nak Nee Haw*...Slum junkie rough heaven! I reside in the receptacle, would you like to remain in the physical? What a dog. There's a girl at Dolphin Square with her green hair; I had to juxtapose ...*Yes, yes,* and "girls" speak as if to bark at me and right in front of me in "The Tulip Caf." Yes, yes. I live in a shape world. Yeah, so basically...she gets loads of photos of herself taken when she barked at me a couple of days ago! And the birds fly for me, for me only... can I have a studio...

The Earth is flat my friend, when you know that you know everything there is to know about the world! *"I hate psychiatry."* Without me there's no heaven, so to speak, but yeah- why does my shadow look not real and yours does, rank off !! And Ram-on! So to speak in Uropa. My computer's- my computer's called *"Magritte"*. And then I thought I was a dog chained up in a hard place to be. And I did the "I like Prake" dance down Uppfel Street. And here I am…fearing that I have to somehow be in another country all the time!

<u>Anne came… 'ere we go!</u>

Some guy just tried to scare me, by putting a key in my key hole. And now…at 14.45pm according to the meridian line, I opened the post. I will like increase your capability to be, my dear; as you function; I thought in cooperation to the computer. Sometimes it stinks-I- what you're not allowed to do- "Penile cars, my red lipstick in Lorenzo's curved and dainty hand" I am in a self containment unit for one person yet I can't get out! God to me, as they say *is not fear*- God is "good". WTF. Stop instilling God…(gravel's really hard for my feet) I don't want to die. You breathe/ I breathe.

<u>24/04/100</u>

How was the football? There are no stars tonight. No-one's higher than the Queen's are. And in Lauder's they hate me…there are no stars tonight and I decided- I hate you Tyronne. Manu- and I took two hours. There are no squares. All my friends were fuckin' squares. No-one's calling—and all the entire global history…I entered with...a black dog. It used to smell of orange blossom in this room twenty nine, I realised I was page eight of eight and I had written 1,765 words. I went out and brought. I went out and brought a social reality check, cough, cough so to speak, in an inchoate lingo. And so then came the "*I swim in my head ; too*" men.

I said *nicely* to a guy... "Copper's daughter...water's chopper."

Basically Dom John would you bite back if that's "*Girl in the bear skin suit*" then the Nutter's choice is better (as a painting). What am I supposed to subsist on-cheese and carrots...? As God's swear. Dad, the craziness is that you were a saint.

There aren't any stars in the sky tonight. When I close my eyes I see cars and loads of birds. And you go mad a little before you sleep then you travel.

At 23.15pm: *"Vade's War,*
God's a black man"

But man, how's the football. Sterility is invisibility, it is so cold. All the women hate you! You masturbate under your coats. "Hindu/ Bindu me not."

There's a boring bit in every book so they brought out highly polished cars despite the fact there's only one star in the sky tonight. Thali you're not an angel, I have walked the Earth in this land of onion and mince meat. We argued but why can't men and women accept the fact that I am holy? *Like* my father, overused, totally hurt

Extracts from an "on the road" diary I kept... You have every single idea of what I've witnessed. A wet foot print along Syrop's Hill where I reckon they have a euthanasia centre. Joe's you worship a religion that renders your children totally incapacitated.

And Muscle's render me totally incapacitated when they walk past me especially the men and women who are covered in disdain. *Maaan*, oh man, so much has happened to me. I walk everywhere. You do a crime and wear a giant golf ball macerated clitoris to a palace and walk in! Evil little comma that you are. Lamb Chowzer I speak inside people, I understand every strand of politics except total ignorance...of me, Ella. Go and sit inside my body and experience the 'Thing'! I mean, "*Eye love you*".

I uncrossed my legs in that little room, and they hurt people.

This is not a jest I'm scared I'm going to die. The weakest of the weak, the most lecherous of the leches. I walk in Flip-Flops under a sky, in a city that has panes of pain- of twinkly lights, that glitter and no one looks up at the skies.

I was muffled until I danced where they sewed wild flowers in Hapsdown Fields near Shears Guild bridge: there is someone famous. I find more in common with the others...the "*oiseaux*"- what can't write birds?!

The people I witness in my head...the people. This morning it took me five hours to find my cigarettes. Lesbos Verruca, and it was spoken down Silver Street. I have flown before. Today is Thursday or something. Englenike library is awful. I need to relax... Wind this up for you, but my book is named after the bird that flew past my window and whispered "Espiritus Sanctus".

Quite frankly; after I got the lotion for my foot! I started the day at 8.00am, bad day to go out, in this Kingdom, currently, Blow-away Road's a long walk.

My writing has been played with, it broke down, that is my computer did. I live at Shiresdown. Yesterday the whole of the communal living space of this bungalow of a Borough thought... or *had it* thought that I would kill myself? I found it deeply upsetting that I was dropping things and people touched me to notify me that I had dropped things. Man, woman and child you'll never see me naked. You took the piss Housebound Street.

I went down the city today past all the suburban shops that must make one feel so at *home* ! And I wept in the shopping centre after I put my coat on and watched a beat-boxer in the square. I walked home to this "White Letter Flat" and kept my eyes down. And kept my eyes. Kept my eyes to the icey paving stones. And saw the people stumble unable to react- even to walk properly without their convex minds fixed on "THERE THINK TANK MOVEMENT-GIRL" I, Ella.

In Ingle-nook...in Englenike. Then I got myself down to a concert called 'Riot' and I walked home with my eyes down cast, laughing down the alley. They're not pigeon feathers that I collect, for I am a captive bird.

THE END

About the author

Sophie Adams was born in Paris, France and lived in Paris. She has also lived in Tunisia, and the U.K and the U.S. She graduated from the Slade School of Fine Art; U.C.L, London and did part of her degree in the U.S at the School of the Art Institute of Chicago, Illinois. She holds a master's in visual arts awarded by the University of Sussex. She writes and paints and enjoys yoga.